About the author

J.D. Maguire is a novelist, scriptwriter and short story writer. He lives in Cambuslang, Glasgow, and worked as a teacher of English at Bellshill Academy for twenty years, where he ran an adult creative writing class.

This is a work of fiction. Names, characters, businesses, places, events and incidents are either the products of the author's imagination or are used in a fictitious manner. Any resemblance to actual persons, living or dead, or actual events is purely coincidental.

ELECTION: RETURN TO GRÀDH

J.D. Maguire

ELECTION: RETURN TO GRÀDH

Vanguard Press

VANGUARD PAPERBACK

© Copyright 2022
J.D. Maguire

The right of J.D. Maguire to be identified as author of
this work has been asserted by him in accordance with the
Copyright, Designs and Patents Act 1988.

All Rights Reserved

No reproduction, copy or transmission of this publication
may be made without written permission.
No paragraph of this publication may be reproduced,
copied or transmitted save with the written permission of the
publisher, or in accordance with the provisions
of the Copyright Act 1956 (as amended).

Any person who commits any unauthorised act in relation to
this publication may be liable to criminal
prosecution and civil claims for damages.

A CIP catalogue record for this title is
available from the British Library.

ISBN 978-1-80016-495-6

Vanguard Press is an imprint of
Pegasus Elliot Mackenzie Publishers Ltd.
www.pegasuspublishers.com

First Published in 2022

Vanguard Press
Sheraton House Castle Park
Cambridge England

Printed & Bound in Great Britain

Dedication

For Beth

Love to: Kevin, Lesley, Megan, Ross, Catherine, Luke, Connor, Joseph and Sammy.

Acknowledgements

Thanks to David Maguire and Jacqueline Stewart

All at Pegasus Publishing, especially Phil Clinker
for his expertise and patience.

Chapter One

The door opened and the narrow back room exploded into silence. The group at the rear, who were sat around two short, square wooden tables pushed together, stood immediately. They took it in turns to pat the burly man, with the slicked-back grey hair, on his back: some offered encouragement; some offered congratulations. He paused as he passed two men who had been standing silently drinking tea from plastic cups. He locked eyes with the shorter of the two and they nodded politely to each other, before he continued towards the door. Eventually, everyone, apart from the two men with the plastic cups, had left the room. The shorter of the two took one last sip from his cup and laid it down quietly on the nearest table. He began to head towards the open door when the other man spoke.

"You looked disappointed... when the door opened. Still hoping?"

He half-turned and smiled ruefully. "When we haven't got hope..."

He turned again and went through the doorway, out into the corridor.

Chapter Two

Four Months Earlier

Harry Swain sat in his office and stared at the front page of *The Post*: a picture of Opposition leader Greg Chance drinking from a large cup with his name on it during a pre-election visit to a factory in Lancashire. Emblazoned across the photograph were the words *Would You Take A Chance On This Mug?* The Editor shook his head. Who the hell let him have his photograph taken in this pose? This was too easy. That wasn't just his opinion; the polls backed him. A crap Government with an even crapper Opposition. This just wasn't fun any more. Not only that, there was another four months of *it* to go.

He sighed, stood and gathered up the notes and emails that had been thrown onto his desk, and headed towards the door to the main office. As he reached it, he turned around and walked wearily back to his desk. He had almost forgotten the email sent from the Seychelles in the middle of the night. A favour for Sir Reginald. He let out a scornful laugh. A favour. He headed back out towards the main room.

He looked around. Not bad. There was a fair bit of activity – which was good. On the other hand, most of his key reporters – his prize bloodhounds – were on the premises – that wasn't good. How to galvanise them? How to galvanise a readership? How to galvanise a nation?

"Right, children. Into the hub."

Swain led the way to a glass room which ran alongside the main newsroom. It had one long rectangular table inside, and he collapsed onto the chair at its top. Various sub-editors and senior reporters traipsed after him and took up their positions on the other seats. Everyone looked bored. Empty. Worst of all, everyone looked complacent. Swain was many things; he was not a fool. He needed to reinvigorate these men and two women. He needed to reinvigorate Harry Swain.

He suddenly pushed back his chair and stood, looking at his audience. He brought both fists down hard on the glass table and looked searchingly at the group. Some straightened up. Others shifted uncomfortably. All paid attention.

He spoke softly: "Children."

He spoke loudly: "What the fuck is going on here?"

Softly: "I know the current apathy was not born here."

Loudly: "But by fuck the disease has certainly spread quickly *to* here."

Softly: "The good news, children, is that we have a cure. Not just a cure for here."

Loudly: "Oh, no. We have a cure for the whole fucking nation. We are the antidote to this fucking disease. And we don't need any bent pharmaceutical crowd, either. *The Post will be* the cure."

The 'children' were lapping it up now. All around were murmurings of support for their Daddy. He caught the eye of Eve Morgan – Agony Aunt – and the way she looked at him, as well as the stirring he felt in his groin, suggested that there would be some executive relief provided on his mahogany table when the meeting ended.

He faced all the group again.

Softly: "This is the run-in to a General Election."

Loudly: "You know that thing when we waste time and energy voting for a bunch of parasites and emotional cripples?"

Everyone was nodding.

"Well, let's give these publicity-loving fuckwits the attention they crave. Let's show the public – our public – what these pricks and prickesses are like. They'll be taxing the arse off you and me and the world and his tarts soon enough. Let's retaliate first."

He stood back and watched the 'table' turn to each other: nodding and agreeing; already planning and plotting. Time to push on.

"We'll decide if this Election is sexy or not. Not the politicians and certainly not the people. They'll do what we tell them."

He looked at them seriously. "So, what have we got? Ian?"

"Story doing the rounds about some Tory Peer – touch of the old kiddyfiddles, if you'll pardon the pun."

Some encouragement from his colleagues, but most looked towards Swain before committing.

"C'mon Ian. That's been done to death. We need to move with the times."

The Editor realised that he had been too quick. No one was willing to engage now, and he hadn't made his own – Sir Reginald's – pitch yet.

"But thanks, Ian. You're on the right track."

He smiled softly at them: the understanding father.

"Margaret?"

Margaret fidgeted in her seat. "Well… there's a Labour candidate running in the North-East." She looked around, hoping for support, but found that no one – apart from Swain – was making eye-contact with her. "It may be nothing… might be something…"

Swain was in supportive mode now. "I'm sure it will be, Margaret. Let's hear it." The others now nodded encouragingly towards her.

"He's into cleavage sex in a big way. Apparently."

Silence.

"I love it. That's the sort of thing I'm after."

Now there was enthusiasm. The type that seemed to charge the air. Everyone was talking to each other. Everyone was overflowing with ideas. Swain smiled indulgently for a short time, then held up his right hand as if commanding the traffic of words to stop.

"Good, people. That's it. That's what I'm after. Now, I want you to go back to your desks and get me more of the same. It's time to set a huge bloody fire under this General Election."

As soon as he had finished speaking, the children rose and began to head towards the door.

Swain raised his right hand again. And lied.

"I'm sorry, folks. I almost forgot." He motioned for everyone to sit back down.

"Got a good one here. A runner. Real good story." He had their full attention. "This is a tale of the underdog. The returning hero. We have an opportunity to help this hero. And, at the same time, help out Sir Reginald." He still had their attention, but some were wary at the very moment the proprietor's name was mentioned.

"Where is it?"

He knew they were on to him, but he had to play out the charade. "Where, Tony?"

"Yeah, where is this story?"

Swain knew that his time was up. "Scotland."

The babble had returned, but it wasn't of an enthusiastic nature any more. Tony spoke again. "You can't send anyone up there so soon after the Referendum, Boss, they'll lynch us."

The Editor knew he was losing them. He had to work fast.

"Whoa, there. Everyone hold your horses. Let's calm down. There has been a little bit of gerrymandering since the last General Election. Nothing crooked; all above board." The children were listening obediently – if not exactly convincingly – again. "Two larger regions have expanded and have left a little one in the middle. It's an idyll little village. Beautiful. Untainted. The project is very close to the PM's heart. And therefore, boys and girls, it's also very close to Sir Reginald's."

All were listening; no one was biting.

"The place is tiny – it really is. And, according to the most recent polls, it's neck and neck in the race for Westminster. The PM has drafted in a heavyweight – former heavyweight – served this place and the area around it for many years; he's our comeback story. He's our star."

"Who's the other guy?"

"A nobody. But – dangerously – trying to be somebody. Cranking on about social justice. Doesn't like bombing the bastards that blow us up. You know the type. Also, the village has just had a little infestation – of immigrants."

The family were jovial again – but still no volunteers.

"This little village. This beautiful, unsullied little place, is our Britain. This is what our brave boys – and girls – die for. Now it's our turn to do something. It's time not to ask what we can do... no... no... it's not the time to ask what Britain can do for us, but what we can do for Britain." He let his last comment sink in for a few seconds, then asked, "Now. Who fancies creating history during the next four weeks?"

A hand went up, three seats from the front, on his left-hand side. "Where is it?"

"Gràdh."

A hand immediately shot up from the end of the table, on his right-hand side. "I'll go."

"Good man. I'll get travel and accommodation details to you shortly. Now, let's get back to work and save this great bloody country." The group headed for the exit: focused now. "Oh, and Eve, could I see you in my office for five minutes?"

Chapter Three

As the two men made their way along the long corridor of the old village hall, the first man stopped and reached into his right-hand jacket pocket.

"Are you okay?"

"Yeah. I'm just gonna try one more time."

Further on up the corridor, a young lady in t-shirt and jeans appeared and shouted cheerily towards the two males.

"They're ready to go. Just waiting on you. It's so exciting."

The man with the phone held against his ear smiled in the girl's direction and gave her the thumbs-up. He had made contact with the mobile phone that he was attempting to reach, but it was ringing out. And ringing out. Eventually, it moved onto message mode, but he 'hung up' at that point and resumed walking in the young female's direction.

"Let's go."

Chapter Four

Four Months Earlier

She stifled a laugh as she watched him tiptoe into the bathroom and quietly close the door. After several seconds, she heard the toilet flush and the wash basin tap turn on. Teeth getting done. Then the shower switch. Bit of a creature of habit, my man. *My man*. She liked that. My God, she almost blushed a little to herself. A year they'd been together. Well, not quite. They'd met about a year ago, lived together for the last four months, and she'd been... happy. She wasn't sure if that word was strong enough. If happy really told everything about how good she felt. How safe she felt. Safe. Was that a word to be used when talking about affairs of the heart? Well, to her it was. It was important to her. Especially as she hadn't felt like that at any time during the previous ten years. And it was fun. Christ, she hadn't been prepared to laugh as much as she had this last year. He took everything so seriously – apart from himself. She sighed to herself. Life was good. What did she want now? For it to continue just the way it was. And that made her sad. Because life has a habit of interrupting.

The bathroom door opened. "Sorry did I wake you?"

Samantha Munn looked out from her office window towards the red, all-weather synthetic running track and the lush green soccer field that was encircled by it. Beyond was a line of trees and then another playing field, this one for rugby. The scene was idyllic: a beautiful, fresh spring morning. At least it looked like spring. Maybe it was still winter. A cough brought her thoughts back inside the room and she turned to face the two men sitting on the other side of her mahogany desk. She leaned back against the window ledge.

"Bert…"

"Me?"

"Yes, Bert Two."

"I want you to see Mark King before lunch time…"

"Mark King?"

"Yes. It's about last night's…"

Bert One straightened up on his chair and looked on awkwardly, but he didn't speak.

"In History?"

The Headteacher's patience was wearing thin. "Yes! Mark King. M-a-r-k-K-i-n-g in History. Okay? I want you…"

Bert One grimaced; Bert Two spoke. "It's...
It's…"

"For the love of Christ, what is it?"

Bert One saw a 'window'. "Dunc King."

The Headteacher fixed her eyes *on* him.
"What?"

"It's Dunc King. In History. Not Mark King.
That's what the kids…" He caught the stare. "The
students… the students call Mr King, Mark. That's
not his name, though…"

She turned her attention back to Bert Two. "I
want you to visit him at the end of the day."

"He's off Period…"

"May I continue?" Both men shifted
awkwardly now. "I want you – Mr Steele – to visit
Mr King at the end of the day." She paused and
looked at the two Deputy Heads sitting before her.
There were no questions. "I want you to tell him
that Mr Barker felt that the penultimate song that
he played last night was inappropriate."

Albert Lyon – Bert One – felt emboldened
enough to speak again. "Are you sure? I spoke to
Mr Barker and the rest of the School Board last
night…" He stopped. The *look* was enough.

She turned her gaze to Bert Two once again.
"We weren't happy. Make sure he understands."

The two men nodded, stood up, then turned and
headed for the door. She called after them and they
stopped. "It'll be better coming from you. Good for

your image. It's always best that the troops understand: the General is a gentleman and the Sergeant Major is a bastard."

The two men made their way along the long corridor in silence. They then went through double swing doors leading to the stairwell. Once they had reached the bottom of the stairs, and gone through another set of swing doors, Steele spoke. "Can you remember what the penultimate song was that Dunc sang last night?"

"Haven't a clue."

"Shit."

He pulled up outside Burns Newsagents at seven a.m. When he opened the door, he was met – as always – by a cheery cackle from Agnes Barr. "Good morning, Your Grace." He laughed – as always – and checked how she and everything else in her world was. "I think the sooner you win this election, the better. Then you can sell up and move to Westminster on your huge salary."

He laughed again.

"Seriously, it's dead." She put on her serious face. "How's your dad?"

"Not so good. I'm heading up there this morning." He looked around the place and felt a pang of guilt. The village was bigger than it had ever been. Surely, logically, more people, more sales? Agnes read his mind.

"Murup! They all shop there. Have done for the last seven years. You've lasted well. Longer than Ryan's and Taylor's: people get their bread and butcher meat under the one roof. And papers." She had wandered through to the small back room and switched on the silver kettle. "Still off the sugar?" He nodded. "I mean, they come from Pleasant and East Deckert for their shopping; stands to reason that Gràdh folk are going to go, too."

She was right, of course. His father had been stopped suddenly two years previously, while the shop was already in steep decline. He was just annoyed that, as his father lay dying, he hadn't been able to arrest the shop's decline in fortune.

"Adams was back in yesterday. Yeah. Looking for you. He's got a couple of ideas… for the shop."

Sean Burns shrugged his shoulders. Bill Adams was a success. He was 'new' to the area. He was the man who built the houses when the village expanded. Some quality housing, too. Many left Pleasant, East Deckert and beyond, such was the enticing beauty of their surroundings – and comfortable commuting distance to the major towns and cities. Sean's father Bobby actually quite liked Adams. He felt that, unlike a good many that he didn't care for, he had a bit of personality about him, and he couldn't argue with his business acumen. He appreciated, too, that his offers to buy were exactly that: offers. At a fair price, too. There was never any rancour on his part, and he always accepted Bobby's 'decision' with good grace. Even when Bobby revealed the reason why he would always turn him down – on the grounds that he was 'big business'. As far as Sean – and Agnes – could see, he was genuinely concerned about Burns senior's illness. In fact, Sean had been surprised – and suspicious – to walk into the hospice two weeks ago to see him sitting at his father's bedside. A quick look at the smile of sheer bedevilment on his father's face quickly dispelled his worries: the old man was thoroughly enjoying the visit. When Sean sat down beside them, he almost immediately realised that the two men were actually friends. As they wished each other goodbye, Adams made another 'bid' for the shop and was met by a two-fingered salute from Bobby. He turned and headed towards the door, spluttering with laughter as he left the room. Agnes had 'run' the shop for the last two months, and Sean occasionally helped out. Bill Adams visited the store on a daily basis, buying a newspaper and cigars. On the rare times Sean had been there during one of his visits, he, too, had found him engaging company. He never commented on the shop; he only enquired after his father's health. So why did he want to speak to *him* now?

He was pretty sure he'd viewed this scene before: in a film or television or something. The nurse was directing him from the main building towards a bench that looked out over beautiful green grass, which seemed to roll on and on and on. The figure, already seated there and wrapped up against the crisp morning air, seemed to be ignoring the stunning scenery and was looking at the ground. He thanked the nurse and headed towards the bench and sat down beside the patient. "Good morning, Justin. How are you?"

Steele paused outside the classroom door. He could see that Mr King was sitting at a student desk with two female pupils on the opposite side. A textbook was open and he was obviously directing the two towards the piece where the correct answer could be found. He checked his watch. He could see that all three people inside the classroom were engrossed in conversation, but he had guitar lessons to take at home that evening. So he took a deep breath, tapped on the door and went inside.

"Erm… Mr King, could I have a word?"

Duncan King looked up from his book which contained Past Papers from previous Higher History examinations. "As long as it's a quick word, Bert…" The two fifth-year girls giggled. "As long as it's a quick word, Mr Steele; the girls are here…"

"Of course. Of course. A minute is all I'll need." The two parties then looked at each other rather awkwardly in silence for several seconds.

"Well, what is it Ber... Mr Steele?"

"Oh, right. In private?"

The History teacher apologised to the two female students and motioned for Mr Steele to follow him towards the door of an adjoining classroom. Once inside, King pulled out a plastic chair from one of the tables for Steele to sit down. He then positioned himself on top of the table opposite. Steele shifted uncomfortably, twisting one way in his chair, then another, before he finally stood up. Still he didn't speak.

"Look, Bert, I'm kinda busy here. Any chance?"

"Of course. Of course. Firstly, I want to say just how much I enjoyed your set last night."

King eased himself off the table and walked towards the classroom door. "That is very kind of you, Bert. I appreciate it, but... the girls." He nodded towards his own classroom and opened the door as if to shepherd Steele out.

"Oh, sorry, Duncan... Dunc. There is something else."

"Oh." King made a great show of closing the door over-silently, then slowly returning to his previous position on the desk.

"It's Samantha. Well, that's not strictly true. Samantha received a complaint last night."

"What about?"

"Em… you, I'm afraid."

"Me? Who did?"

"The School Board."

"The School Board?"

"Well, not the School Board exactly."

"What?"

"Tom Barker."

"Tom Barker? That obsequious, fat prat. Christ Almighty, what a…"

"Now Mr Barker is a hard-working…"

"Tommy Barker is a loathsome toad who probably tosses himself off every night to that picture of him and his pin up – the *Headie* – in *The Post*. Bloody hell, Mark Twain had it right."

"Mr Twain?"

King shook his head. "It doesn't matter. What on earth is the complaint about?"

"Your songs."

"My songs?"

"Song."

"A song? Which one?"

"The one about…"

King detected hesitancy on Steele's part. "The one about what?"

Steele's face was red now and he was fidgeting a great deal. "The second last one."

"Which *one*?"

The game was up. King was totally calm now. "Do you know which one?"

"Well…"

"Mr Steele. Do you know the name of the song that I played last night – around seven hours after my 'shift' ended – that so infuriated our pillar of the community?"

Steele grimaced again but didn't speak.

"Would it be too much of me to ask you to find out which song I sang which upset our esteemed School Board Leader? If you could do that, then I might just be able to give you my thoughts on the matter."

Steele stood up quickly, attempting to regain his composure. "I don't appreciate your tone. Please watch the way that you are speaking to me."

"What?"

"You have been warned regarding your conduct, Mr King. I do not believe that there is anything else to be said." Job done, Steele spun around and immediately stumbled over the chair that he had originally been sitting on. He stood to his full height and pushed at it, but one of the legs caught on the other chair at that desk and would not move. He then pulled at it, but it was still entangled, and now both chairs lay on the floor. Eventually, he negotiated his way beyond the two stricken chairs and reached the door. He turned once again to face the ever incredulous-looking Mr King.

"And now I must bring this particular discussion to an end. I have an important business meeting that I must attend." For extra effect, he slammed the adjoining class door shut with great force. Such force that the square of glass that it contained, cracked, then fell dramatically to the floor. Mr Steele did not look back.

Chapter Five

The man sat upright on his red leather lounge chair. The television blared and glared back at him as he stared towards it. On the small wooden table to his left, a light shone. Not from the table lamp – which had not been switched on – but from the mobile phone lying there. He did not move to answer it. If he noticed the brief flash of light or the gentle vibration of the phone, he gave no indication.

Chapter Six

Four Months Earlier

He couldn't even be sure that the man he shared the bench with was listening. It seemed that, regardless of the topic, he was simply unable to penetrate whatever sort of invisible shield it was that surrounded the other man's mind. He wasn't even fifty yet – not close – and here he was, incapable of any sort of response. The body was still in good shape – he was getting plenty of exercise – but he was an empty shell.

David Tait recognised the figure walking towards him. It had been around two years since he had last seen him. Once, they had been friends; next, they had been in-laws; and then, well then, they were friends again. They shook hands warmly, as old friends do. The time apart immediately dissolved as both reminisced about past times and past friends. Strangely, to anyone witnessing the discussion, this trip down memory lane did not feature the one person who, legally at least, bound them together. Perhaps blood wasn't so strong, after all.

He helped the elder man to his feet, made sure that he was comfortable, and then took his left arm in his right hand as they walked along the path surrounded by the rich, bright greens. When they eventually arrived at the fence's end, he steadied his companion and lifted the piece of metal which was attached to the gate and draped over a square green post. Once outside, he again made sure that the other man was secure, before replacing the metal back in its place. The two men continued on their way along the path, the younger of the two talking about every topic the two had – used to have – in common: family, acquaintances, football, holidays, news. It didn't matter. Regardless of the topic: one talked; one listened – maybe. They came to another bench, this one overlooking the placid blue water of the lake. Again, he made sure the other man was comfortable.

"Debbie and the kids are asking for you. She's going to visit you next time she's down this way. Phil is still travelling everywhere, of course, doing very well. Although it wouldn't matter if he wasn't; my sister loves him, and that's it."

Still nothing. No recognition at the mention of his favourite niece.

"I've got to go away for a few months."
Nothing.
"The Election is coming up."
Nothing.

"The boss wants me to head up to one of these constituencies that's still in the balance. Create a bit of interest. Create a bit of... mayhem." He laughed. "You know what it's like. You should do – you taught me. I guess, if it's not already there, I'm going to create a bit of news. Give old Joe Public what he wants. What he craves. Isn't that what you always taught me?"

Nothing.

"So, tomorrow, I'm heading up..."

He noticed that the other man was no longer looking at the ground, but out over the lake. It seemed stupid, but it was almost as if his uncle was bracing himself for what was to come.

"... to Scotland. To..."

Justin Meade turned his head from the lake and looked directly at him. He then started to slowly shake his head from one side to the other. He avoided his uncle's gaze for a few moments before he looked back at him. Then he nodded once.

The two men had settled for a coffee at the 'local' franchise store: one of the benefits of a growing village and an influx of money. "I can't believe there's a Café Bella here in Gràdh. I hope it's not against your principles, David, but I ain't setting foot in The Village. Not just now. Probably not ever again."

David Tait smiled. "Those are my principles, and if you don't like them…"

"Well, I have others." They both laughed. "Groucho was right."

"Exactly. I find that – in my sixty-first year – grey is a very acceptable colour. So, here is just fine." Tait studied the man across from him again. "And Joan? The kids?"

"They are great. Joan and I are off to Seattle next month. A little bit of business, but mostly fun. Young Kevin is doing very well in the computing world – he's still in New York. We're going to stop over on the way back to visit him. And Yvonne – well, she's just Yvonne. Battling to put the world to rights down in the Big Smoke. Taking on the Fat Cats. I'll know just how well I'm doing if she ever comes after me."

Both looked down as if considering their respective coffees. After what seemed like a minute or two of silence, Tait spoke.

"I'm glad to see you again, Kevin, and I'm even gladder that everything in your garden is so rosy. You've a really lovely family, but if you don't mind me asking, what the hell are you doing back here?"

Harry Swain shook his head. If he was honest, he didn't give a toss about Justin Meade. What the hell was he to him? However, Colin Dyer – Meade's nephew – was sitting across the table from him, and he thought it was the right response. Besides, if *his* man didn't have some morbid fascination about what had happened to his uncle, then he might not have been able to get anyone to go to Gràdh. And he quite liked the kid. He had a good nose for news. Especially *Post* news. "Shame, eh? Just in his fifties, too."

"Forty-four."

"That's even worse. So you're all set?"

"Yeah. I'm getting the mid-day flight and pick up a car in Edinburgh. I've made contact with a local photographer…"

"How local?"

"Don't worry. Local-ish."

Swain smiled. "Good. Last thing we need is someone with split loyalties."

"Exactly. He's freelance. I'll use him when needed."

"Good. Just a little point of information. Their local rag is the *Gràdh and Pleasant Post*…"

The younger man interrupted. "Yeah, I…"

"So, for the first few days, while you are settling in, just let the yokels think you're connected to the local paper. You'll think of something regarding the accent."

Dyer was listening intently now. Lesson learned. A nod from his Editor told him that the conversation was ending. He thanked him, stood and shook Swain's hand when it was offered. He then turned towards the door but stopped when Swain spoke again.

"Oh, one other bit of information. Actually, more motivation than anything else. Our target..."

"Burns?"

"Yeah, well, his father – Burns Senior. He owns the local newsagents. Hasn't carried *The Post* for... well, years."

"A newsagent that doesn't carry the nation's biggest-selling newspaper. Is he retarded?"

"Obviously. Anyway, we're gonna do a few promotions up that way. You know, in the supermarkets and the like. Boost our circulation."

"Sounds great."

"It is. That way we can bury the father and son together."

The two men shook hands again, and then Dyer made his way from the room.

It seemed an age while Kevin Munn contemplated his answer. Tait could only remember one time when they had fallen out. He was so sure. So convinced that Munn was wrong. The arguments never turned towards the physical – they had too much respect for each other, and a blow either way would have caused irreparable damage to their relationship – but they had been fierce. Maybe if he told Kevin that he believed, in the possibility at least, that he might have been wrong. That Kevin Munn might very well have been right. Maybe then his old friend could feel some sort of closure and turn around and head out of Gràdh forever. The two men's eyes met. Both had been thinking back to that same time. Then they began to speak at the same time. Both laughed and, after the verbal equivalent of two people standing on opposite sides of a doorway, beckoning the other through, Munn cut through the silence.

"I had no choice, but you... you... how the hell could you marry her?"

Again, both men stared at each other in silence for a few seconds, before erupting with laughter.

The woman on the other side of the table dropped her large coffee cup onto her saucer and stared in disbelief at her son. Had she heard right? Was he really going to *that* place? Was he really going to be near *that* bitch? Was there something wrong with her son? My god, hadn't he visited her brother often enough to know just how damaged he was? Yet there he was, sitting across from her, looking calm, assured – smug almost. Just like Justin.

"I'm doing it for him, mum. Yeah, I'm going up there on newspaper business, but I want..."

"What? Revenge? Your uncle worked away happily up there for eight years. He was happy working for that local rag; said that he learned a lot.

Then we don't hear from him for about a year and he's broken into television. Going on as if it's some big deal. Then suddenly he's got that *tart* attached to his wagon. I warned him. Warned him. But no, he had to marry her. I say had to… you know what I mean?"

Dyer nodded. He knew, okay. Christ, his mother had told him often enough. But that was the thing. This wasn't a whodunit. This was more of a *how* and a *why?* Hopefully, he would find out over the next few months. However, for now, he would settle for calming his increasingly excitable mother.

"Hey, I've Googled the place. There's even a Café Bella there now."

Tait could hardly disagree with Munn's sentiment. When his then wife had told him she was leaving, he wasn't surprised. Considering his line of work it was perhaps surprising that confrontation wasn't his strong point, but he had known for some time that she wasn't happy. He had known for some time that she had *moved on* –mentally, at least. He *was* surprised to discover that she had moved on physically, too. He hadn't noticed much difference there. Not in terms of quality or quantity. In fact, when Boy Wonder was having his breakdown, he always seemed to be ranting on about how "cold" she was. *Only in her heart*, Tait had thought, *only in her heart.* He looked up again at the man opposite.

"Never mind about her. Any chance of you answering the question?"

"Ha! David, it really is good to see you again. I'm so sorry for the time when we didn't speak. You were always a good…"

"Whoa. Steady. We've known each other for fifty-odd years. For a couple of those we didn't speak. I know we don't see each other much these days, but we can – and we have – picked up the phone for the occasional natter. We know where each other is. We know that when either of us wants anything, the other is there. I think, as friendships go, we've done pretty well."

Munn's demeanour said that he agreed, but paradoxically it also said that not all was right in his world. When he had first walked towards Tait, the latter had thought how tanned and fit he looked. Up close now, though, he could see that he was certainly tanned, but his eyes had… had what? A weariness? Was that it? Maybe. No. His eyes had more of a sadness in them.

"Kevin. Come on. Enough. What is it, man? Why are you here?"

"I'm here to settle an old score. Wipe the slate clean. No regrets. Nothing left behind."

"Left behind?"

"Yeah. I'm dying, David."

"Jesus, Kevin. You always knew how to rain on a parade."

Both men laughed and then held each other's right hand across the table in a tight grip.

Tait composed himself. "Do you know... how long...? Do you know how much time you've got?"

"Enough."

The flight to Edinburgh had been called and he made his way to the departure gate, pulling his boarding pass from the front of his black and yellow flight bag. He noted that he was fifth from the front, when he felt a sharp finger push under the sleeve of his t-shirt against his bare left arm. He turned to see a short, blonde-haired, attractive young lady with a puzzled look on her face, open out both hands in a silent plea for an explanation.

"Oh. Hi. I thought you weren't due until tonight?"

"Obviously."

"Got some work." He nodded in the direction of the British Airways crew, who were collecting, then tearing off and returning, passengers' boarding cards. He let two couples go in front of him, then produced a shrug towards the female that suggested it was time to go. He hesitated one last time and turned back towards her.

"How did the...?"

"The funeral. How did my mother's funeral go?"

By now he was past the desk and heading towards the walkway, leading to the plane. "Yes."

"It was *great*. Absolutely *fan-tastic*."

Just before he disappeared from view, he gave the thumbs-up. Then he was gone. An expletive from somewhere behind him was fired but, by the time it reached him, it was barely audible.

Chapter Seven

Still the phone rang. Still the man sat motionless. Still he stared impassively ahead.

Chapter Eight

Three Months Earlier

Mr Quinn was trying – desperately – to put across his love of Shakespeare to his third-year secondary class. He wanted them to appreciate. Engage. Empathise. Involve themselves. However, resistance was strong. He thought that showing the award-winning film alongside the words of the Bard would reap dividends. Yet two boys were now referring to a major character as *The Wee Jew*. A girl – whose father was a major fan of *The Godfather* film – kept referring to the same character as *Michael*. Not only that, he wished that he had saved a pound coin every time one of the students had confessed to surprise that colour film had been around in *Willie's* day. Just as he signalled to the class to lift up their text books, a knock on his classroom door was followed by a fair-haired boy – whom he knew from First Year – sticking his head around the door. At first, the young lad said nothing, producing stifled giggles from the classroom members. Eventually, Mr Quinn spoke. "Well?"

"Can Jillian Gibb go…?"

"No."

The boy looked dumbfounded. "But…"

"Jillian Gibb cannot go anywhere from this classroom."

"Eh?"

"Jillian Gibb cannot – at this time – go anywhere from this classroom."

"But…"

"Do you know why Jillian Gibb cannot go – quiet class – anywhere from this classroom, at this precise moment?"

"'Cause she's at the toilet?"

Cue hysteria from the assembled students. Mr Quinn had to use all of his years of practice of the *threatening stare* to achieve silence once more. He turned again to the perplexed-looking boy, who was now standing inside the classroom, though still holding the door ajar, as if keeping his escape options open.

"No, she's not at the toilet. In fact, she's not here in this class…"

This time it was the boy who interrupted and, in doing so, he was afforded no rebuke.

"It's just that Miss, sorry, Ms Munn wants to see her." Jesus, thought Mr Quinn, the Evil Witch herself. I hope I haven't kept her waiting.

"This is a Third-Year class. Miss Gibb is in Fifth Year. You will find her in Room 40 – at the end of the corridor."

Confused at the sudden outpouring of information, the boy remained rooted to the spot.

"Well?"

The student shrugged, turned around and made his way from the room.

"Now, why are Jews so unpopular at this time?"

"Because of the way they treat the Pales..."

"In the play. In the play."

Jillian Gibb made her way along the long, pristine corridor. The shy boy who had come to fetch her had already ducked into the classroom which he had been plucked from. More accurately, Ms Munn had secured his services while he had been out of that class and heading towards the boys' toilets. He was glad of the break. He quite enjoyed Religious and Moral Education as a subject, but all too often the class teacher – Mr Lyon – was missing. He always seemed to be present at school, just rarely in his classroom.

Jillian climbed the stairs slowly. An invite to the Headteacher's office was not an occasion to be celebrated. When she reached the top of the stairs, though, it dawned on her that was a bit of a sweeping, if not downright inaccurate, statement. She had never, never been summoned to the Headteacher's office before. She had seen others sitting in trepidation on the seats outside it, awaiting punishment for some particularly heinous crime. She had seen others – like her good friend Lisa Caldwell – sitting outside in their smart black blazers with navy blue braiding, awaiting the call to discuss the latest project to promote the school. As she pushed through the double glass doors at the top of the stairwell, she tried to recall if she – the Headteacher – had ever actually talked to her – on a one-to-one basis – before. She turned to her left and saw that the first door she came to, on her right-hand side, was open. Miss Grace, the Headteacher's secretary, viewed the young girl suspiciously.

"Do not come into this office. Stay in the corridor, go through the next set of double doors and sit on one of the two chairs outside Miss Munn's office. You will be informed when to enter."

Jillian offered a *thank-you*, but the older lady had already resumed whatever writing task she had been working on when she had arrived. As she took *her* seat, she focused more on the reasons for this *meeting*. She certainly couldn't remember doing anything out of the ordinary – good or bad. She was never at the top in any of her subjects at school, but she did decently across the board. *Consistent* was the term applied to her in her most recent report card. Even in History. At one time, that *had* been a struggle for her. She could remember dates and could list various famous occasions, but she had difficulty analysing them in the greater scheme of things. But, throughout last term and this, she had attended Supported Study with Mr King, and the improvement was there for all to see. Again, not the best in class, but decent. At this rate, she would achieve good passes in all of the eight Higher Examinations that she would attempt. Not great; but good. Consistent. Supported study with Mr King...

Her line of thought was broken momentarily, as she was now aware of voices. In fact, there was one voice that she recognised easily: that of Lisa Caldwell. It was coming from inside Ms Munn's office. Jillian began to relax because, while she struggled to pick up on actual words, she recognised a happy tone to her friend's voice. Just as one or two words began to form, the door to the office opened and a cheerful Mr Lyon *showed* a smiling Lisa from the room. There was no time for communication between the two girls, but Lisa's grin confirmed to Jillian that all was well with the world. As her friend pushed through the glass doors, turned to her right and disappeared along the corridor, a beaming Mr Lyon held the door open wide, before welcoming the young student into the Headteacher's office.

Duncan King was having one of those strange moments. He knew, deep down, that it was a Tuesday. He knew, deep down, that the clock on the wall was correct. The time really was 3.55 p.m. Yet he repeatedly checked the wall clock and his *Family Guy* desk calendar. Supported Study was, as ever, on offer. However, unusually, no one appeared to be taking up the *offer*. His numbers had been up and down throughout the year, peaking at seven just before the Prelim Examination. That was normal. Kids who hadn't done much work throughout the year were suddenly gripped by panic and tried to cram as much study and preparation as they possibly could over a very short space of time. However, regardless of how the numbers fluctuated throughout both terms so far, there was always a constant. Two constants, to be more precise: Lisa Caldwell and Jillian Gibb. Since the new school year had begun, they had been there – without fail – every Tuesday after school. Occasionally, they were joined by others, but he could set the wall clock by them – usually.

Lisa Caldwell he knew best of all. She was an intelligent, witty and thoroughly enthusiastic student. He didn't 'go' Mrs Caldwell, Lisa's mother, much. He'd always thought her a bit of a 'big-mouth'. She was on the School Board and tended to spend her daughter's information evenings 'working the room', as opposed to hearing about Lisa's progress. Maybe she just had confidence in her daughter's ability. And why not? Lisa had been in *his* second top Third-Year class. Her work during that year had developed to such an extent that she was 'promoted' – as he was – to the top class during the following certificate year. Her 'A' pass duly arrived, and now she was thriving in the all-important Fifth Year. Her good friend, Jillian Gibb, was already in the top Fourth-Year class when he took over. She was a steady, if unspectacular, worker. Good enough for the top section – just. She had achieved a 'C' grade at the end of that year, and he was unsure that she could cope with the greater demands of *Higher* work. However, his Principal Teacher had argued her case for inclusion, and the girl herself had promised to work harder – and attend Supported Study. Mr King had to admit they had been proved right. Jillian was as good as her word as far as attendance and additional work was concerned. She was still a 'C' level student, but at the more difficult level, and – with a bit of luck on the day – she might even climb to a 'B'. He looked towards the clock again – still no girls.

Strangely, when the adjoining classroom door window had been broken three weeks ago, he had been a little angry when he had returned to help them with their studies and he was concerned that the girls might be upset and not show the following week. But they had. And the week after that, too. Maybe he'd need to watch them a bit more closely. He wouldn't want them becoming complacent just as the finishing line was in sight.

When Jillian entered the spacious room, the Headteacher, although she must have been aware of the schoolgirl's presence, was busy scribbling furiously on a piece of paper on her desk. The sound of Mr Lyon closing the wooden door was the cue for her to look up from her *paperwork*. Then she rose, walked around the wide, oak desk and embraced the stunned schoolgirl warmly. Ms Munn didn't speak, she just smiled at Jillian. The student couldn't quite 'read' what the smile meant, but it seemed to fall somewhere between understanding and pity. Still without speaking, the Headteacher led the youngster towards two cream-coloured couches, facing each other, on the left-hand side of the impressive desk. A low, rectangular glass table separated them both, and Mr Lyon sat on the one nearest the door, while Jillian sat in the centre of the one opposite. Ms Munn sat down next to her, on her right, leant forward and squeezed the girl's two hands, which were clasped together on her knees, with her left hand. Then, in a voice scarcely above a whisper, she spoke.

"How are you?"

Jillian began to think that Ms Munn and Mr Lyon had sent for the wrong girl. She looked back into the Headteacher's sympathetic eyes and answered, "I'm fine."

Ms Munn turned her attention to her deputy.

"Did you hear that? She's fine. Isn't that what I'm always saying, Bert?"

He didn't know where this part of the conversation was heading, but Mr Lyon was already nodding his head vigorously in agreement.

"We produce the very best students…"

"Ye…" Too soon.

"The very best citizens of the future. Determined. Brilliant. Emotional when need be, stoical when necessary."

There was a rather anxious silence as Mr Lyon tried to ascertain if he should speak now. A widening of his boss's eyes told him that it was.

"Yes. Very much… Samantha. You're always saying that."

Watching the Headteacher's look of sincerity reminded Jillian of the old news footage she had seen of former Prime Minister Margaret Thatcher's Saint Francis of Assisi speech. Ms Munn spoke again.

"Mr Lyon – Bert – and I are so sorry that this has happened to you. I want to stress that while we, as a school, naturally focus on academic brilliance, your safety – *your safety* – is of paramount importance to us." She smiled again – even more sincerely – and looked towards Mr Lyon, who nodded, then smiled, and then, at one point, with great effort, did both at the same time.

"I cannot begin to tell you how sorry we both are... how sorry all the staff are."

There was another pause and Jillian smiled, hoping that some thought would emerge within her mind that would help explain to her just what on earth these two crazies were going on about. Still no one spoke, and finally the young student really did feel that the time had arrived to question just what it was that had 'wounded' her so gravely.

Chapter Nine

There was no one else to be seen, but he could sense an impatience beyond the long corridor. Again, he dialled the number. Again, it rang out. Again, it went on to voice message.

Chapter Ten

Three Months Earlier

He wasn't sure why he chose this location, but at times like this he always did. The walk from the car park, through the forest to look over the sprawling green fields, was always beautiful. That's what he told himself. And why not? Anyone standing where he was right now would immediately confirm his prognosis. In time, like always, he would continue his way along the pathway, but he always stopped at this particular tree and offered a silent prayer. Today, he continued the tradition, but said another for Bobby Burns, whose funeral he had attended earlier in the day. Was it really twelve years ago?

Almost. He remembered exiting Carol Ann's cottage and seeing the newsagent consoling a distraught Ian Moyes. There had been two deaths that day: one immediate; another which didn't reach its denouement until two years later. However, there was no doubt when the decline began. Until then, he had never seen such a mountain of a man disintegrate so rapidly. Mind you, at the beginning, throughout his mournful mood, he kept a close eye on me – and Justin Meade. He wanted to be sure that her name was not going to appear anywhere. Not on television; not in the newspapers. Once he was satisfied, his descent began in earnest. His secret had gone with him to the grave. Ian Moyes didn't know that David Tait knew the farmer's secret. It didn't matter. The chief reporter, editor, photographer and headline writer of the *Gràdh and Pleasant Post* had made a decision almost twelve years ago, and he had never – not for a second – regretted it. *His* secret would go with him to *his* grave also.

Sean Burns was sitting with those oxymoronic emotions: loss and pride. It had been just him and his father since he was ten. His abiding memory of that time was coming down from his bedroom late at night for a glass of milk, about a month after the funeral, and seeing through the open door of the family living room, his father sitting in a chair, staring into space. Occasionally, a shimmer of light from the silent television would illuminate his father's face and he could see a rivulet from each eye run down his cheeks. Instinctively, he knew that his father wouldn't want to be discovered like this. The strength, the show of strength, ever since his mother had been diagnosed, was for her, and was now continuing for his son. Sean tip-toed back upstairs. When he reached the top, he stamped loudly, then began to make his way back down again. He was greeted by his clear-faced and smiling father before he reached the bottom. Once his father had cheerfully attended to his needs, he had asked if he could stay downstairs for a little while, as he was feeling a little poorly. His father agreed immediately and made a little bed with a blanket and pillows on the couch for them both. As Burns senior held his arm around him, Sean could sense his father relax, and this in turn made the boy pleased. For once, at least, *he'd* helped his *old man*. Sitting now in the suite of the hotel, he smiled at the memory – oblivious to the other mourners – and held his glass high in a silent toast to the finest man he'd ever known. *Fooled you once, Dad. Just the once.*

Sean spotted Bill Adams and Alana looking towards him. He couldn't hear any words, but he realised that the businessman was bidding her farewell. He stood up from his chair and they shared a tender embrace. "I'm sorry…"

"You have to go?"

"I'm so sorry, but the Headteacher…"

"Hey, I know."

She kissed him on the lips and turned to go away. He held onto her gently.

"Thanks."

"For what?"

"For loving him."

"Don't be silly. He was easy to love." She kissed him again, and this time moved away. After a few steps, she stopped and turned around. "I suppose that's the way with all of the Burns' males?" They both laughed and then she was gone.

Sean turned to shake the hands of an old aunt and uncle – his mother's sister and her husband – who were also ready to take their leave. Once he had seen them to the door, he spotted Bill Adams, with two generously filled glasses, heading in his direction. Adams handed one of the single malts to Sean. Before he could speak, though, the younger man started. "Bill, I know you've been looking for me. Agnes was saying…"

Adams' demeanour changed completely. "Son, I was a *friend* of your father's. If you think I've been chasing after you behind his back and then seeking you out at his funeral…"

"Bill, stop. Please. I know you were… a friend, that is. Look, I can only apologise, I'm …"

"No need. Someone that Bobby Burns vouches for – and he was always praising you – has got enough credit left in the bank." Adams could always 'read' people well, and he could see that the man opposite him now was genuinely concerned that he *had* offended. "However, although today is not ideal, we do need to talk. Okay?"

The younger man nodded. "Of course. And, Bill…"

"It's forgotten. I know you've got enough on your plate today, so tend to everyone and everything else in here first. I'll speak to you at the end. If it wasn't important, I wouldn't impose."

"I know. I'm sor…"

"Stop. Forgotten." With that, Adams meandered off to join another group. Sean stared after him. No wonder his father liked him. Strong. Blunt. Genuine.

The walk from The Village to Gràdh High School was around ten minutes. She was enjoying the soft breeze against her face. As she entered the school ground, she considered the emotions that she had. She was sad. Obviously. Not just for Sean, but for her. Yes, he had lost his father, but she had lost a great friend. Warm. Kind. Generous. Welcoming. God yeah, welcoming. She'd never forget that. Discovering his son had been a *godsend*, something so good. But then? Then she had met his dad, and my god she had discovered there were two of them. Not two Burns'. Two fantastic human beings. Two reasons why she now, after so much darkness, enjoyed life; couldn't wait for the next chapter. Now one of those lovely, beautiful reasons was gone. And that was why she felt sad. However, deep down, she felt so satisfied that she had known this person. He might indeed be gone, but he had shown her that there was indeed light in this life, too. She would always be grateful for that.

When she reached the stairs leading to the main entrance of the school, she was aware of two figures – one male, one female – standing just inside the glass doors. The Headteacher, shaking the man's hand warmly, she recognised. By the time she had climbed the dozen steps, the stranger had emerged from the building. She reckoned he was under six foot, had short, styled brown hair. At a guess, she figured him to be in his late twenties, early thirties. As he approached her, she thought that he was looking as if he knew her. She couldn't place him. A student's parent, no doubt. As they passed, she cheerily greeted him with a smile and a "Good afternoon".

He smiled back, continued walking, and responded, "Good afternoon, Mrs Osbourne."

Although her left hand was already on the long, wooden frame to open the door, she stopped and looked back at the man. He never broke his stride, just continued to walk towards the school car park. She opened the door and shook her head, dismissing any notion that something weird had just happened. She was being stupid. After all, Osbourne *was* still her name. Besides, although she always announced herself as Miss, students – particularly the young ones – would occasionally call her Mrs by mistake. Maybe she just imagined it. His walk never slowed or faltered in terms of his gait, but she had been pretty sure that there was a definite pause before the word "Mrs". Crazy? No doubt. In fact, she was now convinced that she was being paranoid. As she headed towards the internal stairway, the Headteacher emerged from the school office.

"Did the funeral *go* okay?"

"Yes, thank you. In fact..."

"That's good." The conversation was ended, and the two females continued their walk to the first floor in silence. Alana Osbourne smiled and began to head along the corridor to her classroom. She stopped, though, and turned back, calling after the Headteacher, who had begun her ascent of the next flight of stairs.

"Ms Munn?"

The Headteacher stopped, stared in the direction that she was facing for a few seconds, sighed loudly and then turned slowly and deliberately. "Yes?"

"That man who just left?"

"What about him?"

"Is he a parent?"

"No. He's from the *Post*."

"Oh. David Tait's taken someone on, has he?"

The Headteacher sighed even more audibly this time and forced herself to produce one of her best patronising smiles. "No, dear. Not the local rag. *The Post*. He's here for the election and is speaking to the important people – the high-flyers in Gràdh."

With that, she turned and continued her ascent. Alana Osbourne wasn't moving, though. In fact, she was still standing at the same spot. Still staring in the same direction, towards where Ms Munn had stood seconds earlier. But she wasn't thinking about her boss. She was thinking about *that* man and *that* pause.

The cleaning staff were now involved in *operation function suite clean-up* as Sean Burns settled the costs with The Village's manager, Tommy White. He thanked him for all the staff's efforts in making sure that his father had an appropriate send-off. Then, following Burns senior's military-style instructions, he left money behind the bar so that the *workers* could enjoy a drink when they finished their shift. Knowing that he was meeting Bill Adams in the public bar, White was surprised to see Sean head for the exit, rather than go through the doors that separated the two rooms. "Thanks, Tommy. I'm just going to get a breath of fresh air."

He stood in the doorway and took a deep breath. He looked up to the heavens and smiled: sad yet satisfied. Today had gone well. When the numbness wore off, then he'd really feel the grief. But today? Yeah, the old man would've enjoyed it.

He looked at his phone to check the time. Alana would be finished by now.

He stepped out onto the pavement and began to walk the fifty or so yards to the main bar's entrance. As he did so, he was aware of a man in a brown leather jacket and jeans, who had been leaning against the wall of the public house, suddenly straighten up and walk in his direction. He also saw a group of four smokers who were huddled together at the side of the doorway. He recognised the three men and the woman as *nodding* acquaintances, and it was as he smiled and negotiated his way around them that he felt the phone in his right trouser pocket vibrate. As he was fumbling to retrieve the phone, the man in the brown leather jacket called after him.

Bill Adams stopped nursing his malt, drank it and returned to the bar. He recognised the attractive young female who was serving him as one of the barmaids who had been working in the function suite earlier. When thanking her for his change and telling her to take *one herself*, he enquired if the funeral next door was *still going*. When she told him it had ended around fifteen minutes ago, he was surprised. Cradling his newly bought malt whisky, he headed back to his table. Where was young Sean? Had he just gone home? Surely not?

He then spotted one of the *smokers* coming back inside.

For whatever reason, the man appeared quite animated and looked to be passing on some story to the remainder of the group who had stayed inside. Adams assumed that something big was happening on the streets of Gràdh. Maybe someone had grown a record-breaking-sized tomato – or something. Whatever it was, he decided that it was best ignored, and began seriously considering emptying the contents of his glass into the one he had purchased for Sean. Just then, the Public Bar's door opened and Burns junior walked in. Adams thought that he looked pale – not unusual under the circumstances – but then he noticed that the clutch of people who had been sitting with th*e smoker* were all looking at his friend as he headed towards him.

Shit. He should have told. Just blurted it out. Made sure he'd heard. Made sure he'd been warned. Shit. Not a week without his dad, and he had left him vulnerable. When he reached the table, Sean was looking at the floor. Adams knew. Adams knew that he knew. He stood up and – too late – he began to speak. Sean looked up and nodded.

"I know. I already know."

Chapter Eleven

He was moving towards the quiet murmur at the corridor's end, but that didn't stop him ringing again. No automated answer service this time. Just ringing out. A young woman held open the door for him and, as he passed her, he placed the phone in his right trouser pocket. Still on. Still ringing out.

Chapter Twelve

Three Months Earlier

Harry Swain had the mobile phone at his right ear within seconds. He knew the call was important, and he'd paved the way the day before. So he listened to the tale. Yes, the Headteacher had greeted his reporter with real enthusiasm; yes, she was delighted to grant him an 'audience'; yes, he had been warmly welcomed; yes, most importantly, she had invited *his* man to today's visit to the school by the two prospective Members of Parliament who wished to represent Gràdh. Not only that, the cheeky young man had 'ambushed' the *target* last night. A pre-emptive strike, as it were. Clever. Throw the enemy off-guard. Let him know just who he's dealing with here. He thanked his man for the call and congratulated him on his fine work so far. As he put the phone away inside his black suit jacket, he realised that the Humanist had stopped speaking. He nodded, walked towards the chief gravedigger and accepted a handful of soil from a small container, which he then threw onto the coffin. As he turned away from the grave, one of the mourners held out his right hand. "She was a lovely woman, your mother, Harry." Swain shook his hand warmly and nodded.

Samantha Munn was in her element. Her two Deputies watched as she strode purposefully around the room. They were delighted with the news. Both beamed at each other as the Headteacher told how Colin Dyer of *The Post*, not the mind-numbing local one aimed at vegetable growers and vegetables, had visited yesterday. He was here, primarily, to cover the battle for the new *seat* in the General Election but wanted a taste of life in Gràdh. Apparently, everyone in Britain, and some people further afield, had been captivated by our not-so-little village. This was an opportunity to showcase the Gràdh community, particularly the school community.

She went on to explain that she had invited Mr Dyer to today's event: Mr Lord and Burns were both invited to speak with the Press after the welcoming address from Ms Munn to the new 'Syrian' family whose daughter and son were being enrolled at the school. Suddenly, Mr Lyon looked perplexed.

"What is it, Bert One?"

"Where will we sit him? I don't have any more…"

Munn sighed loudly. "Is it possible we have one more chair in the building?"

"Yes, but not the good ones."

She considered this for a moment. "Get another plastic chair from the nearest classroom. Add it at the end of the first row." Mr Lyon nodded, and both men rose, ready to take their leave. "Oh, that will spoil the look." Both men now nodded at their Headteacher, who appeared lost in thought. "I know. Put the other plastic chair with those at the back row and have Tait sit there. Colin, Mr Dyer, can have *his* seat at the front." Both men were happy again and turned to leave the room, only to hear Munn yell at them to wait. The meeting was not quite concluded. "I almost forgot. What colour are Syrians?"

It was the fourth time that morning that Alana had visited Miss Grace, the Headteacher's secretary, in an attempt to see Ms Munn. All requests, including this latest effort, were politely, but firmly, declined. She had hoped to catch up with her before the start of school, but, despite arriving at her usual time of eight a.m., she discovered that she had 'missed' the Headteacher, who was – unusually – already at her desk. The other abnormality of the morning was that Miss Grace was also in position at that time, ready to fend off any unwelcome intruders. She really needed to speak to her boss before the Press arrived. However, no matter how much she pleaded her case and the importance of it, the Headteacher's

Rottweiler was unmoved. She had her instructions, and those instructions would be followed. Another three visits had been made in the knowledge that the welcoming ceremony was going to take place after the mid-morning break.

The two men sat in the deserted Munn Suite. One studied the man opposite him and wondered if the Party was taking this Seat a little too much for granted. He thought that he saw something in the old warrior's eyes that appeared to suggest that this was maybe one battle too many. Would it be that bad if he lost? Hell, he really liked the other guy anyway. However, old habits die hard. He liked the man he was sharing coffee with, too, and he'd known him an awful long time. Besides, in his experience, it was generally beneficial to himself – both personally and in business terms – if the Party triumphed. The other man saw that he was being studied. "What is it, Bill? What's so urgent?"

"Something happened after you left yesterday."

"Bobby Burns' funeral?"

"Yeah. I got a tip-off a couple of weeks ago from a business associate down in London. He was seeing his wife on a plane to Edinburgh and there was a couple arguing in the queue. He thought it was quite funny; then he heard the name Gràdh and gave me a phone."

"I don't get it. What's the connection between your pal and Bobby Burns?"

"My associate recognised the guy heading for the plane as a reporter for *The Post*. I smelled a rat straight away: election time, and he's heading to the back of beyond. Anyway, he turned up yesterday looking for Sean. At his old fella's funeral." Adams studied the other man's eyes. Suddenly full of life. His disappointment was genuine. "Oh, Thomas. You knew."

Thomas Lord took another sip of his latte.

"Politics, Bill. Politics."

She thought back to the early morning rise after an uncomfortable night of tossing and turning. Him, trying to reassure her. Console her. Her, trying to work out just what it all meant. Why on earth would the biggest-selling newspaper in Britain be interested in her? To get at Sean? My God, the electorate was so small in the village, surely it wasn't going to affect the outcome of the General Election? She'd snapped his head off this morning. When he had suggested she stay at home. Now she realised that, he was still wrong, but he just wanted to protect her. She was sorry. Not for being right, but for forgetting about him. That's what this was all about: getting at him. She had thought for a second that he was making the suggestion for her to take the day off to protect himself. She regretted saying it aloud almost as soon as she had spoken the words. She saw the hurt in his face. Trust. *She* still had to learn what it meant.

Duncan King had been in a state of confusion for weeks now. Since Mr Steele's visit to his classroom during Supported Study, he had rarely seen any of the Senior Management Team, and, on the rare occasion that he did, they didn't speak to him and they avoided eye contact with him. Not only that, neither Lisa Caldwell nor Jillian Gibb had been back to his classroom since the episode that culminated in the smashed glass. Not for Supported Study; not for *normal* tuition. He had tried to raise the matter with his own boss – Department Head Brian Gillespie – but he was always too busy to speak. Maybe he was getting a bit paranoid, but Brian had even cancelled a Departmental meeting – for the first time ever – during the same period. He had almost forgotten the reason for Mr Steele's visit in the first place. Almost. About a bloody song.

Bert Steele was just making his way across the corridor, inside the main entrance of the school building, about to begin his climb towards the Headteacher's office, when he noticed a figure, from the corner of his eye, ascending the outside stairs. He stopped and began to head back towards the door. The visitor 'rang' the intercom system, but before anyone in the main school office could respond, Mr Steele shouted, to no one in particular, "Let him in."

The man looked unsure of his destination but was relieved to see Mr Steele standing there. The Deputy watched as the tall, heavy-set man, who was smartly, if casually, dressed, made his way towards him. The black face was all the convincing he needed. *Christ, they're here.*

King thought that he had Steele cornered, but just as he bounded towards the Deputy, another man had stepped into view, and Bert Two was now shaking him warmly by the hand. Regardless, Duncan King pushed on towards both men.

"Good morning, Mr Steele. I wondered if…"

Steele continued with the silent shaking of the stranger's hand and looked angrily at the source of the interruption. "This is not the time, Mr King." He turned back, smiling again, towards the man in front of him.

"Well, I'm sorry about that, *Bert*, but I've been waiting for an opportunity to speak to someone from management for ages now."

Steele stopped shaking the man's hand and released his grip. He bowed once and turned away. He gripped King around the right elbow and led him about six paces away to the side wall of the main office.

"Can't you see that I'm shaking a black man's hand?"

Duncan King could only stare at him. Then he spoke softly. "I'm drowning here, Bert. What's going on?" Steele shook his head. King was pleading now. "For old time's sake?"

Steele met his eyes for some seconds, looking as if he might well respond, but then he turned away and walked the few paces back to the visitor. He twisted his wrist and pointed towards himself.

"I. Mr Steele. I. Happy. To. Meet. You. Hello. And. Welcome. To. Gràdh. High. School." He then performed a strange half-bow and began shaking the man's hand again.

The man flashed an impatient grin. "Thank. You. Now, where the fuck do you want me to put the flowers I've got in the van for you?"

Just then, Samantha Munn swept downstairs towards the main entrance, in the company of a man, a woman and two young teenagers. "Bert Two. Come and meet our lovely Syrian family."

David Tait parked his red Mini and walked towards the main entrance to the school. He saw a young man pacing up and down outside the building with his mobile phone to his ear. He actually stopped for a moment, thinking that he recognised the distant figure. He began walking again, realising that unless he had travelled back through time, it couldn't possibly have been whom he thought it was. As he ascended the last group of stairs, he saw the man enter the school building. Once inside, he noticed him pull something small but bulkier than a mobile phone from his pocket. He saw the man being greeted warmly by Deputy Bert Lyon and led into the main assembly hall. Then it dawned on him. The package the man had pulled from his pocket was some sort of mobile recording device, and *he* was the elusive *Post* journalist who had been darting around the neighbourhood this last few weeks, gaining the trust of the locals and posting tame village life stories for his newspaper. Tait was suspicious. A simple search on Google had revealed that Colin Dyer was one of the *Post*'s top writers. He couldn't just be here for cute, furry animal stories, could he? And he was here today. At Gràdh High School. When a Syrian family was being welcomed into the fold and the two front runners for the Gràdh Seat at the General Election were speaking? He followed the small throng, making his way to his normal seat in the front row. Before he reached the front, Deputy Steele stepped in front of him. "Your seat is at the rear today, Mr Tait."

He was about to respond when he noticed Colin Dyer with his head turned, smiling in his direction.

"It's okay, Mr Steele. I understand." With that, he turned and headed towards his new position: at the end of the last row – eight from the front.

Chapter Thirteen

He looked down from the small platform across the sea of faces. Dazed. Still no sign. He pulled the phone half out of his jacket pocket and dialled. Again.

Chapter Fourteen

Three Months Earlier

Another restless night. She sat up in bed. Six o'clock. Any last pretence of even attempting to sleep was over. She heard him move around the kitchen. First filling the kettle with water, then switching it on. She moved along the short hallway through to the small lounge, just as he emerged with two piping hot mugs of tea. She sat down silently on one of the chairs. He handed her the one that said *Free Palestine*, while he held onto the one which had a picture of *Lois* from *Family Guy* on it. He sat down on the edge of the couch on her left-hand side and leaned forward. Holding his mug in his left hand, he gently ran his right hand down the side of her face. She tried to force a smile, but stopped, noticing that he wasn't just upset about yesterday. There was something else.

Almost twelve years ago. Remarkable. He didn't think that he'd come out the other side. Her death hit him hard. He loved her. Genuinely loved her. Then those bastards at *The Post* found out. Then that prick Meade, on *Sky*. Hounds after a bone.

Somebody had tipped them off. Somebody that didn't know who. How ridiculous was that? *Married MP In Secret Love Trysts*. Ha, but no other name. Just mine. Just mine. What seemed like half the world's media camped outside his front gate for days, then she killed herself. No, *they* killed her. For hours, then days afterwards, sitting tight. Waiting for the phone call from... from someone. Anyone. Someone that had put the simple equation together. And what was easier than one plus one? But the call never came. Two days after her death, they all left. Television. The Press. Just as suddenly as they had arrived. Nevertheless, having once been tipped for *the* top job himself one day, he knew that his invite to Downing Street this time around was not because the Prime Minister was concerned about his health. *A period of stability* was mentioned. *Let things blow over. You'll be back.* Well, now he was. *They* needed him. Not the other way round. Someone with experience, know-how, call it what you will, but if this upstart Burns was to be beaten, they needed someone with *it*. And guess what? After eleven years out in the cold, that someone was him.

The Headteacher began scribbling on a piece of blank paper as soon as she heard Alana Osbourne touch the door handle from the outside. Even after the teacher had entered the spacious office and closed the door behind her, she continued to look down, scribbling furiously. As Alana made her way towards the large oak desk that the Headteacher was sitting at, Samantha Munn lifted her head so abruptly it was as if she had been interrupted while discovering the original manuscript containing Beethoven's 7th Symphony. She quickly rose from her chair and walked around the table to greet – and embrace – this female member of her staff. Alana felt somewhat relieved when the short hug ended.

Munn broke away slightly and ushered her towards the more comfortable couches. "Please, my dear, sit down over here. It's much more comfortable."

Alana did as she was told, moving up the couch facing the office door, when she realised that the Headteacher was intent on sitting down beside her. She had already spotted a copy of *The Post*, lying on the glass table in the middle of the surrounding seats. Munn didn't speak. She just smiled weakly and allowed her eyes to move from teacher to newspaper. Alana thought that she was waiting for her to say something. However, the second she took a breath to begin, Munn spoke.

"You poor girl. How terrible for you."

"Well, to be honest, it's not nice, but…"

"Having your dirty laundry on public display, as it were."

Alana looked at her quizzically.

"About your affair."

She tried to compose herself but found that she couldn't speak. Her Headteacher had no such problem. "I was *furious* with Mr Dyer when he asked Mr Burns about the two of you in front of the children." Again, Alana tried to speak, but found that words were trapped in the back of her throat. "But later on he explained – and I'm still not best pleased, mind – that what public figures get up to in their personal lives affects us all." With that, she stood up and walked back towards her desk. She picked up the phone. "Miss Grace, would you be so kind as to come in and help... Mrs Osbourne leave? Thank you."

Alana struggled to her feet, unsure of exactly what had happened. She didn't even notice the school secretary enter the room, but now she felt her guide her towards the open door. Maybe it was the short waft of air, or maybe it was the contact with another human; either way, something acted like a splash of cold water across her face and she pulled away from the secretary at the doorway.

"My name is still *Ms* Osbourne. I should have changed back to my maiden name when I left... when I escaped from that monster. Not just my title. I didn't want to confuse the kids. I didn't want to make a fuss. How stupid I am. When I *was Mrs* Osbourne, you used to look the other way when you passed me in the corridor with my thick make-up barely covering my bruises. You never even spoke. Yet you knew. You bloody knew."

Samantha Munn pulled her best *shocked* face from the vast reservoir contained in her head for disquieting moments like this. "Now, dear. Don't swear. Let's not make this already tricky situation worse."

The two men sat on the park bench, enjoying the spring morning and yesterday's triumph. The younger one, sitting on the left side, was there to bring the other up to date. To reassure. To praise. "The PM was delighted with your performance yesterday."

"Really?"

"Don't sound so surprised, Thomas. He's delighted. He always thought Chadwick was far too hasty in showing you the door. Especially after it had all blown over."

Thomas Lord smiled. Yes, he had been rather good yesterday. All the good habits had come flooding back. He'd rehearsed the scene often enough, but you just don't know. Not until it's actually happening. Yet there he was. In the eye of the storm and taking charge. The mock surprise when that vile little toad Dyer ambushed his target. The appeal for calm. The regret as he scolded the nation's media and reassured the voters that this was not the reason for the two candidates' visit to the school. Oh, no. They had come, along with many in the community, to welcome *our* new Syrian family to Gràdh. Yes, he had noticed dozens of protesters – he counted five – on the way into the school, and no, he did not agree with them – but he did understand their concerns. Unlike Mr Burns. Christ, he was so rattled he even thanked me for my public support. Very kind of him, really. Maybe this race wasn't going to be so close after all. "He didn't take my calls. When he first got in."

"Just waiting for the right time, Thomas. Just waiting for the right time." There was a silence. "The PM went out on a limb, you know. You weren't a unanimous choice. Not by any manner of means." He patted Lord just above his left knee. "Now he's going to have two superb MPs in very close proximity. It's going to send a very powerful message to the country." The man stood and looked down at Lord. "Anything you need, you call me. Understood?" Before he could move off, Lord spoke.

"You're new. Relatively speaking. Yet you know why the previous MP dumped me?"

The other man was speaking softly now. "I do indeed, Thomas. It was simply because the PM felt that it was necessary. Don't worry. That story is known only by a trusted few and is buried – deep."

Thomas Lord watched him walk away. Another *shadowy* man. If their ideas are so great, then why don't they stand up and shout them out in front of everyone? Just like he had done. Just like he had done – once.

Bill Adams was not a man who felt awkward in any company, yet he felt that way today. He was angrier with himself more than anything else. He'd tried to warn Sean: attempted visits; attempted phone calls. Yes, Young Burns was partly to blame because he had been avoiding him. True, it had been a flawed decision by his friend's son, but hardly surprising. He was fighting an election, after all, and dealing with a dying father. No. Adams felt *he* was to blame; and after the events of yesterday, he felt even worse. As he entered the shop, a quick glance at the newspapers piled on the counter and the headline *Now 97*, did little to alleviate his mood. However, if Sean bore him any ill will, he appeared to be hiding it well, as he headed towards him from the back of the newsagents. "Bill. Good to see you."

"Is it?"

Burns laughed. "Always. C'mon through to the *office*." He spotted Mrs Barr raise her eyebrows. "Tea, Agnes?"

"If you've got time."

Both men laughed, but Sean still took her hot mug to her at the shop counter before any discussion began. When he returned to the small storage room, Adams was sitting on one of the two chairs and leaning despondently against the diminutive wooden table. "Bill, will you relax, for Christ sake? It's not your fault."

The other man seemed unconvinced. "I suppose you've worked out that that bastard Lord knew?"

Sean nodded. "Yeah. That's why I thanked him publicly for his support yesterday. Play the game and all that."

Adams was shaking his head hard. "If only there was something we had on him. I'd let the bastard…"

Sean spoke quietly but firmly. "Whoa, Bill. I'm pissed, too. Particularly for poor Alana having to go through all of this crap; but I don't want to know anything about him. It's of no value to me. I won't be using anything about him personally."

The older man tried to interrupt. "But…"

"But nothing, Bill. I can't be telling everyone about a bright, beautiful tomorrow if I act the same as him. I've got to be different from him. And the bloody *Post*."

"It's going to get nasty. It's going to get nasty for Alana. There'll be more to come if that scumbag Dyer is crawling around Gràdh."

"She, I *will* have to protect. But I'm not going to throw away any principles that *I* have, because other people don't have any. Yes, Gràdh needs to trust me, but I need to trust Gràdh."

"Even if you lose?"

"Even if I lose."

Adams shook his head and picked up his mug of tea and took a long sip. "What is it with you Burns'? Are you all fucking mad?"

Sean laughed and held his own mug towards the businessman, who giggled like a naughty child as he clinked his own against it.

The man had been sitting across from him for fifteen minutes. They had discussed the previous day's event, although only the newspaper man had actually been present. Both agreed that the 'ambush' on Sean Burns had been brutal and uncalled for. At first, David Tait thought that the man perhaps had some concerns that the *Gràdh & Pleasant Post* had been in on this personal attack or had some knowledge that it was going to happen. However, during the course of their conversation, it was becoming apparent that this was not the case. The man certainly seemed to be harbouring some sort of resentment that went further than the national newspaper's tacky attempt at smearing Sean Burns as some sort of home wrecker. When a lull in the conversation arrived, Tait looked at the man and waited. Years of experience had taught him that sometimes it was best not to rush. The man was looking downwards, as if studying his shoes, when he finally cut through the silence.

"I don't know what to do. There's no Unions in there, of course. I don't know where, or whom, to turn."

Tait nodded as if he understood. An assurance that when he was ready to continue, the reporter would be listening. "It's serious. Very serious." He looked up, eyes tired and bloodshot. "I've been accused of sexual misconduct. By a pupil."

Chapter Fifteen

"Ladies and Gentlemen. The result of the election of the Gràdh constituency is as follows…"

Chapter Sixteen

One Month Earlier

His eyes passed over the offers displayed in the front windows of the Murup supermarket. The store was always brightly lit, and he could see other posters inside, on the top of various goods, at the beginning of the four visible aisles, highlighting very generous offers. What were they called again? A lost leader? A false leader? Maybe a loss leader? Something like that, anyway. He would have continued to debate this important matter with himself, had he not seen his 'target' emerge from the large store alongside his wife, who was pushing a full trolley of goods.

The man spotted him, and then smiled in his direction, but he ignored him and walked on ahead of his wife. The newspaper man did not shout after the two, but simply followed until they slowed at the rear of their Audi Quattro. The man, aware of the approaching Tait, pressed the 'unlock' button and walked to the front of the car, leaving his disgruntled wife to lift the hatch-door on her own and begin loading the various goods from the trolley. She needn't have worried. Her knight in shining armour was on the scene within seconds.

"Hi, Norma. Can you manage those yourself?"

"Hello, David. Barely." She made a face and nodded in the direction of her husband, sitting behind the wheel and staring aimlessly beyond the car's windscreen.

"Hello, Tom. I didn't see you there."

Barker, knowing that he was lying, grunted and continued to stare in the same direction. Tait made small talk with Mrs Barker while continuing to help her load the various goods into the ample boot of the car. When all cargo was on board, Tait insisted that he would dispose of the trolley. Although he bade Mrs Barker *goodnight*, he left the trolley immediately behind the car and walked to the right-hand side, bending down to look inside the driver's side window. Although it was impossible not to see him, Barker began to reverse, despite the incredulous look from his wife. He immediately stopped as he felt the rear of the car come into contact with the abandoned trolley. Tait knocked on the side window and waited for some sort of acknowledgement. Eventually, the window was lowered.

"You okay, Tom? I'm sorry, I haven't moved the trolley yet."

Barker smiled through gritted teeth. "Sorry, David, I didn't see you there."

Tait played along with the charade. "How's the kids?"

"Yeah. Good. Great."

"I'm glad I bumped into you, if you pardon the pun," Tait said. Barker's wife noticed her husband's deep intake of breath. "I've heard a wee story that there's a bit of trouble up at the High School."

Before he could reply, Mrs Barker spat, "What's that bitch up to now?"

Tait laughed, but her husband reacted angrily. "Norma!"

Misinterpreting the outburst from Barker, she apologised to Tait. "I'm sorry, David. I didn't mean..."

"It's fine. Not everybody loves her. Eh, Tom?"

Barker stared icily at Tait. "We're busy. We need..."

Tait met the glare and interrupted Barker. "A good man's in trouble up there, Tom, and I'm led to believe it all began with a complaint about a song."

Barker was seething now. "Well, I believe it's a lot more than that now, so..."

"Do you, Tom? You've been informed of developments, have you?"

"As Chairman – Chairperson – of the School Board..."

Once again, Tait cut across him. "What was the song, Tom?"

"What?"

Mrs Barker was endeavouring to find out what was going on, fidgeting and trying to interrupt.

"The song."

"What song?"

Tait looked towards Norma for a moment, then back to Barker. "The song *she* told you to complain about?"

"The song's not important…" This time, Tom Barker interrupted himself. "It was me, I com…"

"About what song?"

Barker pushed on the door and got out of the car, heading towards the abandoned trolley at the rear. Once he had pushed it aside, he shoved past Tait and into the car. He reversed, then had to brake again as the sound of a horn from another vehicle told him that he was almost in trouble. Tait once more bent down and looked inside the car. "See if he can remember, Norma. See if he can remember the song title. Before the *Bitch* has to tell him." At that, the car successfully reversed, then sped off through the car park at high speed.

As Sean made his way up the stairs of his apartment block, he came across Alana standing at the door of the flat underneath their own. Mrs Maxwell was standing in the open doorway beaming brilliantly and handing over a huge bouquet. "There you go, my dear. What a beautiful bunch of flowers. Three this week; you're spoiling her, Sean."

Burns grinned awkwardly towards the widow, while Alana thanked her for taking them in for her. The pair headed silently upstairs. Once they had removed their outdoor jackets inside the flat, Sean broke the building silence. "Three this week?"

"Yes."

"Why didn't you tell me?"

"I knew what you were like when the first one came."

"Yeah. I was angry. Mad. Not at you, though. You didn't think…"

They stared at each other. Both unable to speak. When Alana finally did, her voice was soft. So soft that it was barely audible. "That you'd hit me?" She saw the pain carved into his face and was angry herself now. Angry at *herself*. He'd been her rock this last year. She was wrong not to speak to him. She had told him much worse – and it had helped. *He* had helped. Shit. That bastard had caused her another problem, and she hadn't even seen him. "No. I didn't. Not even for a second." And that *was* the truth.

"Anything else before I go, Mr Adams?"

He looked up, smiled and shook his head at the attractive brunette who was standing in the doorway of his office.

"No, Meagan. Get yourself home."

She began to turn but seemed to think better of it and walked over to the front of his desk. She nodded in the direction of a single white envelope which lay on his desk. Although open, the contents remained inside. "Same as the others?"

"Yeah."

"Some people. I'm sorry, Mr Adams." Her words, like her smile, were warm and generous.

"It's not your fault, Meagan. Now get yourself home." She turned and, once more, headed for the door. This time, it was Bill Adams' words that made her stop. "Do you think I'm right?" The young secretary agonised over a response for some time.

"Honestly?"

"Of course."

"I'm not so sure. But George says we should look after our own. First, anyway!"

Adams smiled wearily. "Thanks again, Meagan. Goodnight."

The newspaper man's eyes scanned the busy town centre bar. Not bad for a Tuesday at six o'clock in East Deckert. Not bad at all. His eyes eventually settled on a bald, slim-built man sitting in a corner of the room nursing a pint of Guinness. As Tait made his way towards him, the man looked up and waved in his direction. When the journalist arrived at the table, the man stood up and, towering over him, offered his hand, which was warmly accepted.

"Good to see you again, David."

"And you, Frank. You're looking good."

The tall man began to edge around the table, but Tait headed him off, pointing towards the near-empty glass. "Same again?" He returned moments later and sat two Guinnesses on the table. After some small talk, the other man turned their attention to the real reason for their meeting. The school had been very helpful. The Headteacher had been particularly keen to help. *Extremely pleasant*, it had been said. The ex-policeman paused for effect and both men smiled: Samantha Munn had fooled another set of 'fans'. The *girl* had obviously been upset. Frank Cook had spoken to both investigating officers – Carla Weir he had known for years. A good cop. Any lapse between the committing of the crime and the actual reporting of it made the case more difficult – but not impossible. They had interviewed both parties. The girl was in a bad way. Obviously upset. King seemed devastated, too. At being accused or caught? It was always difficult to tell. Investigation is ongoing.

"Did they give any inkling of how they felt it might go?"

"As I say, officially the investigation is ongoing, but…"

"What?"

"Well, these guys are experienced in this field. Always difficult with the accused, but you usually get a sense if the victim is on the level. If things, sometimes little things, ring true."

"And?"

"And they got that with this girl. She seemed authentic. It's statutory rape we are talking here because she made it quite clear that she wanted it to happen. Kept saying that she loved him."

The retired policeman noted the look of concern on Tait's face.

"Nothing is set in stone, David. But the thing is, particularly with kids, you get to recognise what's real. The evidence just isn't there in this case, but the girl… Carla Weir reckoned from the girl's description of the act, remember she's not screaming rape. It sounds *real*."

Tait nodded, picked up his, up until then, discarded pint glass and began to take a long drink. The two men talked about more general items of news over another Guinness, then left the bar together. Outside, they shook hands again and headed off along the broad pavement in opposite directions. After about twenty steps, Tait suddenly stopped and turned, but there was no sign of Cook. He had already been swallowed up by the night. He turned again and headed back in his original direction, towards East Deckert's main train station. Just then, he spotted a familiar face walk out the main railway exit. He was about to call out, but the man suddenly veered sharply to his left, entering the second bar outside of the station. Maybe all was not lost for Duncan King. Not just yet, anyway.

Adams arrived at the house that Bill built. Like all in this particular estate in the south of Gràdh, overlooking the stream that meandered lazily towards Loch Pleasant, he was particularly proud. The setting was beautiful and the houses were a standing endorsement of admirable architecture and expert craftsmanship. At least, all the other houses were. At least, all of the rest of this house was. All but the wall he stood in front of. What made people do things like this? What the hell motivated people like *that*?

Once inside, Adams saw Sean Burns was sitting at an oval-shaped, glass dining table alongside David Tait and opposite Dr Azmeh. Although both owners indicated to him to sit down, Adams stood behind the other two visitors. "Dr Azmeh, I'm so sorry. I…"

The doctor stopped him with a raised hand and a smile. "I thought that my husband and I were supposed to call you Bill?"

"Yes…"

"Well, in that case – Bill – would you please do my husband and I the honour of calling us by our first names also?"

As the other Dr Azmeh – who had shown him into the kitchen and was now seated beside his wife – Adams smiled back at both.

"Amna and Malek, I'm so…"

This time he was interrupted by the male Dr Azmeh. "Bill. The only emotion our family feel towards you is that of a profound and everlasting gratitude."

The businessman was surprised to find that he was unable to reply. So, instead, he smiled and took a seat at the curve of the table, on the seat that Dr Azmeh had originally pulled out for him. The group talked about the graffiti on the side of the building. About how sorry the three were. About how ashamed the three felt. Each time it was mentioned, the Azmeh's reiterated that while the incident was obviously regrettable, nothing could take away the many kindnesses they had received in Gràdh since their arrival. When they mentioned this, Adams pushed his hand into his right side suit jacket pocket and rested it on the anonymous letter which threatened to BURN THE MUSLIMS out of their home. He thought that was funny. Strange. They'd actually used the word *home*. Not house or building. Semantics, eh? Anyway, regardless of the terminology, the letter wasn't being shown to the Azmeh's tonight.

David Tait was also enjoying tales of the *good* Gràdh. For him, though, he knew there could be no respite: he would have to tell the assembled company tonight. There was to be a march. Through the Town Centre on Saturday week. A march demanding that the Syrians be thrown out of Gràdh.

Chapter Seventeen

Despite the constant noise from the vibration of the phone on the wooden table, the man still looked straight ahead: trance-like.

Chapter Eighteen

Two Weeks Earlier

He wasn't sure whether or not to take the car. Was there any point? Anyway, he had eventually decided that he would. The streets were fairly sparsely populated on this early Saturday morning. He wondered rather gloomily if that would be the case when the march got underway in a few hours. Why was he feeling *gloomy* about it? Was it a sign? Nevertheless, he pressed on, before coming to a halt on top of Gràdh's only road bridge that crossed over the south- and north- bound motorway. He switched off the ignition. Why? Again, he wasn't sure of the *rules*. So he pulled the keys from the column and pulled the door handle towards him. Outside, he was aware of the slight drizzle falling silently from the sky; but, well, so what? For a moment he thought about moving left or right, before deciding that facing southwards was best. He moved along the bottom of the grass verge, before making his way up the slight incline to his right. At the edge of the grass were grey railings which, he discovered, came up to his chest. On the other side was a small wall compiled of grey bricks.

For reasons best known to himself, he scaled the fence carefully, before sitting comfortably on, legs dangling over, the grey wall. He watched the traffic shoot underneath his feet for a few seconds, before staring into the distance. Suddenly, he appeared to remember something and put his right hand into his jeans' pocket. He then placed the car keys on the wall beside him. He smiled at nothing in particular and then slid from the wall.

David Tait stood outside the front door of his ex-wife's bungalow. Before she had gotten a chance to answer his question, a figure had appeared behind her, carrying a jacket and making a huge show of buttoning up his shirt. She looked at Tait as if slightly embarrassed, while Colin Dyer put his arm around her waist and pulled her awkwardly towards him, giving her a large kiss on the lips. As he broke from her, he grinned at Tait as if expecting some sort of reaction. On noticing that Gràdh's *Post* Man was merely smiling back at him like some understanding, wiser uncle, he quickly trotted down the stairs. If Tait was bluffing, he was damn good at it. Noting that the London newspaper man seemed slightly unsure of himself for once, Tait turned around to fire some sort of broadside in his direction. But he suddenly stopped himself. Dyer was unaware of this change of heart, but Samantha Munn was not. Even when Tait had turned back to face her, she could see that he was still deep in thought. For the second time since Dyer's arrival in the village, Tait had looked at him – and seen someone else.

"If you want to speak to me, I suggest you…" Tait's trance was broken.

"I can't get past Miss Goebbels. But then, I'm sure you know that."

"I can't talk to you about any member of staff, far less one who is under investigation."

"Samantha…" This made Ms Munn take notice. When the hell since the break-up had he ever called her *Samantha*? "What the hell is going on?"

Momentarily caught off-guard, it looked as if she was about to speak. Like the great prize-fighter that she was, though, she was soon off the ropes and back in command, if not of the situation, at least of herself. "As I said, if you want to speak to me about business, then contact the school. Other than that…"

"But this isn't business. This is a man's life. And a young girl's." The impassive look on his ex-wife's face told him that the brief conversation was already nearing its end. However, he tried once more. "C'mon. Dunc King, for God's sake! What did he do? Eh? Park in your car space one day? Don't forget, I know you."

"And I know you. You're never more obnoxious than when you're on some sort of crusade. No wonder you never amounted to anything. Not like…" She stopped herself.

"Justin? That ended well." She was about to speak again, but Tait went on, "At least I've still got some sort of health, unlike most of the men you've come into contact with." He then spun around and began to make his way down the front steps. He stopped at the bottom, still facing away from her. He still had a dilemma. The way Dyer moved. His mannerisms. Should he warn her? He was aware that she hadn't moved from her earlier position, just outside the door. Did she deserve to be warned? Obviously not! He started to move off again. But was he then just as bad as her? He stopped and turned around. She was waiting, as if expecting him to say something. Something cruel. So when he spoke, his tone surprised her. "I know it's not my place to advise you on who you should share a bed with… but… something's not right here. This whole thing… anyway." Again he made to leave. This time she called after him.

"Will you be there this afternoon?"

"The march? Yeah. I'm covering it."

"I'm opening up the school hall for the marchers. Provide tea and coffee."

It was Tait's turn to look astounded. "You are? Don't the KKK or the National Front need it for a coffee morning?"

She shook her head. "Typical. You've got the wrong end of the stick."

"*I* have?"

"Yes. I'm allowing anyone in. Give everyone a chance to calm down. Thomas Lord is going to be there. He'll have a chance to address the…"

"What about Sean Burns?"

"He's been invited. He's not going on the march – of course. He's doing some hippy protest against the protest sort of thing."

"Jesus, Samantha. You really are something else."

"What?"

He shook his head. "What is it? Tea or coffee and scone for 20p?"

"Thirty."

For a few minutes they stood silently. Each looking everywhere, anywhere, but at each other. Eventually, Samantha sighed. "Joan came to see me."

Tait was non-committal. "Yeah?"

"Kevin didn't know, of course. Begged me to take a test and see if I was compatible."

Tait spoke without malice. "Must've been desperate."

"She was."

"Will you?"

"I already have."

She didn't offer any more information, and Tait didn't request any. He nodded and turned to move away. Again he stopped. "About Dunc King. It's time to stop; it's gone too far. You know your problem at that school, Samantha?"

"Could I persuade you to tell me?"

He continued, ignoring the sarcasm in her voice, "You've surrounded yourself with too many idiotic, sycophantic cowards."

Again he turned away, and this time he continued to walk away from her.

Duncan King thought that he'd be seeing black now. He wasn't. All was still light – albeit still with a slight drizzle. It took him a few seconds to comprehend that he – by a giant twist of fate – had landed safely on his back, on top of a lorry. This really was a sign.

Tait decided to leave his car just off Gràdh's main street and follow the polluted procession on foot. He parked on the little side street near Carol Ann Love's old house. In his mind, he corrected himself: her old home. Funny how it still stood. It looked good. If it could talk, what tales would it offer up? Noting that few protesters were outside *The Village* as he had driven past, he allowed himself to drift back to that fatal day: poor Ian Moyes; poor Bobby Burns. He was never really sure if he felt sorrow or pity for Thomas Lord. Yes, he'd felt angry towards him at the time, and many times throughout the years, but he'd reasoned – or maybe Tait had simply excused himself – that Lord must have felt terrible, too. For someone as sweet as Carol Ann to have had feelings for him, he must have felt something for her. And, of course, there was poor Carol Ann herself. He was wakened from his morbid reminiscences by the sight of a figure in his rear-view mirror. He could make out a young female with long black hair, wearing dark jeans with stylish tears at the knees and wearing a green parka jacket, heading towards the pathway that in turn led towards the woods. When she had disappeared from his line of vision, he observed again the incongruously happy-looking house. He suddenly sat upright. The girl. The girl that had just passed by his car and headed towards the woods. The girl was Jillian Gibb.

Tait fairly scrambled from his car and took off down the pathway. Funny what comes to mind. He remembered puffing and panting as he beat a path towards the horrific discovery ten years before. Now here he was, not exactly running – or even jogging – but he was not out of breath. Much. Not quite a *fuck you*, but more of a *take that* to Diabetes 2.

As he emerged from the first cluster of trees, he saw the young girl sitting alone in the small *Love Recreation Park*, on one of the swings. As he opened the small green gate to enter, she glanced up and looked for a moment as if she might take flight. Tait tried his best reassuring smile as he moved towards her. In an attempt to assuage her, he mentioned her name. He wouldn't say that it had quite the effect that he was looking for, but as he got closer to the girl he could see she had been crying. She may not have found his attempt at solace much comfort, but she wore a resigned look that suggested she would not run away either.

"Can we talk?" he asked. The young girl shrugged and looked into the distance. "I'm David Tait. From *The Gràdh and Pleasant Post*."

Now she was off the swing and walking past him at speed. He stumbled after her, pleading, "I'm not here for a story, Jillian." She stopped and turned around. "Not for the newspaper, anyway. I want to talk about Mr King." She stared at him for several seconds as if she was about to speak. Then she shook her head and began to move away again.

Once more he called after her. "Jillian. It's okay. I can help. Together we can fix this."

She spun around. "Fix? We? There is no fixing this."

He moved towards her and spoke gently. "There is a way. Please." She looked at him, tears now streaming down her pale face. He nodded towards a bench, just outside the playground perimeter. She nodded and they walked slowly towards it.

For a while they sat in silence. Her wringing between her hands the linen handkerchief that he had given her for her tears. Him waiting patiently: ready to listen if necessary. She wore her vulnerability like a coat, so he knew that the first words would have to come from her. Eventually, they did.

"It's such a mess. A terrible, terrible mess."

"I know. It has just gathered momentum and now it seems like it's out of control…"

"It *is* out of control. You won't believe me…" She stopped herself. What was the point?

The silence continued for several moments, but Tait was encouraged by the fact that the young girl showed no sign of moving away from him. This time he felt that he could break the silence. "He was in a position of power – and trust. It wasn't your fault."

"It wasn't his either. It wasn't rape. He didn't do anything that I didn't want him to do. He loved, loves, me."

Tait's mind flashed back briefly to his meeting with Frank Cook. How he'd begun to head home that night and how he'd seen Duncan King. "Okay.

I'm sure *he* didn't force himself on you. But *he* should've known better."

"You've said. So what?"

"Well, it is a crime."

"You don't understand anything. You know nothing."

"I know what you already know: that *he* isn't Mr King?"

The young girl's eyes flashed in his direction and she blushed slightly. She caught herself just in time. "Do you? And how do you know that if it's okay to ask?"

Davit Tait met her eyes. "Because, Jillian, Mr King isn't interested in young females. In fact, Mr King isn't interested in females of any age. Not that way." At first, it seemed as if she would protest, but she stopped herself and looked away. "Jillian. I believe you. I believe your story. I really do. Apart from the one undeniable fact – Mr King didn't touch you."

It all came out in a rush: she sobbed; she begged forgiveness; she mentioned Duncan King. No, it hadn't been him. She'd been fed that part of the story, after her pal had panicked and told Ms Munn. But she didn't know who. What did it all mean? She looked up at Tait. She wouldn't drop *him* in it. She'd tell everyone it hadn't been King – but no more than that. She'd protect *him*. That's what this was about. She was sorry about King. So sorry. So sorry for the pain she'd inflicted on him, but she'd go to jail before she mentioned *his* name. Then she cried some more.

Tait listened to it all. There was no point in interrupting her; no point in demanding fresh answers.

When she was done talking, but still sobbing, he put out his left hand and laid it gently on her right arm.

"I'm not asking anything else from you, but I think we should go and put Mr King out of his misery."

She nodded. "You'll come with me?"

"Of course."

They both rose and headed towards the playground exit.

"Am I in trouble?"

"No. You can't be in trouble for putting things right."

He'd jumped. He'd tried to die, but he'd survived. He'd survived, and by god it felt good. He felt elated. Indestructible. He would fight. Clear his name. That much he did know. Standing on the roof of the lorry made him feel like some colossus striding out over the land. His land. Duncan King looked back at the only road bridge in Gràdh that crossed the motorway and laughed. As he turned around, he thought that he'd never felt so alive. He was just in time to see the only rail bridge in Gràdh that crossed the motorway rush towards him.

Chapter Nineteen

He looked down at the carpet. Then he turned his attention to the marks on his hands. He began to open out his fingers and felt his knuckles ache. He stood up and walked towards the small kitchen. For a brief second he paused at the short, square dining table and looked back through the open doorway to the living room carpet. Turning back, he observed the two meals of his favourite dish: steak and roast potatoes. Hardly anything had been eaten from one of the plates, and nothing had been eaten from the other. He made his way around the chair which lay, knocked over, on the ground, and went to the sink. There, he turned on the cold water tap and put both hands under the steady stream. He watched as the blood washed from his knuckles and swirled around the drain, before eventually disappearing.

Chapter Twenty

Two Weeks Earlier

Thomas Lord stood on the stage of the school assembly hall. Of course he understood people's frustrations. Of course he understood that people in Scotland – hell, people in Gràdh – were suffering. Of course he understood that everyone, and he meant everyone, had the right to march – a right to protest. And, of course, he understood the need to look after our own. Always and forever. But he knew Bill Adams. He was a good soul. But this time? Well, this time – a free house, free fittings, etc, etc – he had been a misguided soul. He couldn't have known that the people of Gràdh would be so insulted. No. Bill was just trying to help. His only crime was that he had fixated on the wrong people. Other people. Not his people. Not the soon-to-be Member of Parliament for Gràdh Thomas Lord's people. Wild applause rang out after every line that he delivered. For his pièce de résistance, he stood perfectly still, centre stage. Slowly, he raised his hands, palms outstretched towards his congregation.

"I'm glad that your efforts are being recognised by *The Post*. And when I say *The Post*, I do mean **The** *Post*. They understand the difficulties that you are facing in this so-called modern society. They understand what it is like to be British – and to be forgotten. In this little piece of British Paradise that we call Gràdh, a war is being fought. A war that if the unthinkable was to happen – if we were to lose – then the very fabric of our society would unravel and unravel quickly." There were supportive murmurings from the gathering in front of him now.

"But please, friends. Do not panic. Our future is in your hands. You have all the power. Make sure you do the right thing for Britain; make sure you do the right thing for Gràdh; make sure you do the right thing for you and your children and their children: vote Lord on Thursday week."

The vast majority of the crowd seemed to swoon for a few seconds before they erupted into wild cheering and applause. Lord savoured the moment: waving enthusiastically and shaking hands with those near the front of the stage. Finally, he shook hands with the Headteacher and began to make his way to the stairs at the side of the stage. Maybe he'd been out of the spotlight for too long, or maybe he just wanted the ovation to continue; either way, he headed back to the centre of the stage and held up both hands for silence.

"I just wanted to thank you once again. You have all been so generous. I swear, when I'm elected a week on Thursday, I'll do everything I can to repay your faith in me."

More applause. Another opportunity to leave.

"But, as well as the joy I feel at being among you on such a special and significant day, there is regret, too." A murmur from the multitudes. "Yes, regret. We have a fine gentleman here from Her Majesty's Press: Colin Dyer. Of *The Post*." There was a smattering of applause. There was a further delay as Lord looked out over the sea of faces, vainly seeking out the reporter. He was gone. The crowd – who had been ready to leave – were turning restless. Marching for their basic human rights on a Saturday morning was one thing; but hell, if this overblown, pretentious halfwit didn't shut up soon, he was going to eat into their recreational drinking time. Lord, as ever, sensed the change in mood. "Ladies and gentlemen, I know you have a great many duties to attend to. I really won't keep you any longer than I have to, but I just wanted to point out that while we – Gràdh, that is – have been given the coverage that this monumental election deserves by the London Press; our own newspaper lightweight, David Tait of *The Gràdh and Pleasant Post*, is conspicuous by his absence today. Perhaps he is out crowning this year's Golden Daffodil winner." Now they were back. Now the throng was lapping it up again. Not Thomas Meek, though – last year's Golden Daffodil winner.

"Anyway, that's up to him. Freedom of the Press and all that. But what I really cannot believe, what I cannot quite frankly stomach, is that while the good people of Gràdh are here today fighting for their wee Scottish village and their big British ideals, Sean Burns – prospective Member of Parliament for this beautiful, green land – is not even interested in gracing us with his presence. No doubt if we were marching against the…"

Suddenly, someone was shouting from Lord's left towards the back of the hall. At first he tried to ignore it, but it wouldn't stop. Eventually, he looked up and could just make out the face of Bill Adams. "Sorry, Bill. What is it? Have you something to say?"

"Two things, Mr Lord. Sorry, three. Firstly, you don't half talk some shit." This provoked wild applause from a group of four youths who were standing at the back of the hall on the other side.

Lord himself was nonplussed. To wild cheers, he spoke again. "I'm sorry, Bill, didn't you say three things?"

Adams was equally unflustered. "I did indeed. The second thing was that I'd never waste a vote on you again." This brought fresh hoots of derision from the crowd – but more applause from the four youths.

"I'm sorry to hear that, Bill. How will I survive?" The vast majority of the gathering were with him once again. So he paused, looked out over all of them, before finally looking back towards Adams. "Please don't keep us all in suspense any longer; what's the third thing you have to say?"

"Sean Burns pulled up outside about two minutes ago. Looks like someone has locked the door, because I saw him heading around to the side entrance. Should be here in... oh, here he is."

At that, Burns emerged through the open right-hand door to the Assembly Hall. He seemed determined but flustered. The four youths patted him on the back as he passed, while the rest of the hall aimed boos towards him. He didn't flinch. Just continued towards the stage stairs on Lord's right. Bill Adams pushed his way to the front of the throng, who – because they had begun to leave – had left quite a bit of space between them and the stage. Only a few at the very back had already left; the rest had been stopped dead in their tracks when Thomas Lord had reclaimed centre stage. A move, if the anxious look on his face was anything to go by, was something he now regretted.

Burns' appearance on stage provoked more boos. He immediately went to Lord and shook his hand warmly. "Good to see you, Thomas."

His adversary looked back into his eyes. "Me, you, Sean."

Now at the front centre of the stage, Burns held up his hands in an appeal for calm. It wasn't forthcoming, so he shouted. Loudly.

"I'm sorry I'm so late. I headed into Pleasant this morning and made the mistake of coming back the short distance on the motorway." There was some fresh boos, but nothing substantial, so he was able to drop his voice a little. "Unfortunately, when I eventually made it to the Gràdh side, the police informed me that there had been a fatality." There was more noise, but it was that of concerned citizens.

Someone shouted, "Any idea who, or even how?"

"Sorry, I don't know any more details." Burns looked out over the crowd. "I don't know who it is." He saw that they were quiet now. "I don't know if it's a man or a woman. I don't know if it's a husband or a wife; a father or a mother; a son or a daughter. But I do know – because I can see your faces – that you're concerned. Upset. Your first reaction is one of compassion. You're not thinking, is this person white? Black? Yellow? Red? No one has asked if the person who has died is from Gràdh. Not one of you. Not one of you has demanded to know if this person – someone's father or mother, son or daughter – is from Scotland. You didn't want to check, before you showed your concern, if this poor soul was originally from England, Pakistan or Syria." There was some hoots of derision from the back of the hall, but they were quickly silenced by the vast majority of the gathering. "No. Your concern, before any other, was for this individual and for his or her family. Why? Because we all understand pain. We all understand grief. And whether we like it or not, we are all in this together. Don't ever forget." He looked at the crowd, who were still. "I said at the start, folks, that I was sorry that I had arrived late, but that was only because I wanted to be in the village to protest against this march." This brought loud applause from the five people now at the front of the stage: Bill Adams and the four youths who had protested on their own throughout the march.

One of the men from the main group had come to the front at this and was remonstrating with one of the youngsters, who, in turn, loudly called the man a "fascist pig". The rest of the crowd became restless once more, but Burns spoke quickly and assuredly.

"Let's all calm down, folks. Remember, there are people, probably in our community, receiving devastating news right about now." The murmurs of dissent abated once again.

Burns smiled and nodded towards the elder of the two men. "Am I recognising a family resemblance, Graham?" Graham Moore didn't speak but nodded stern-faced towards Sean Burns. "Well, Mr Moore Junior, your dad is definitely not a pig, and he can't be a very good fascist if he's managed to raise a son with such differing political opinions as himself." The young man was red-faced but laughed, as did some others in the crowd. "Besides, Graham, didn't we – and I'm sure many others did in school, too – used to sit and feel enraged – and I know you were enraged, Graham, because you sat next to me in History – when we read and heard about the Holocaust. We weren't just enraged about the despicable things that man did to his fellow man. We – you and I, Graham – were angry because no one would help. No one would give a voice to those who most needed it."

Another voice was heard from further back. "Things have changed since then."

"Yes, things have changed. We are *now* in a position to help. We can *now* do something to help the very people who need it."

Another voice. "For Christ sake, they've got a bloody house – for nothing. Next it'll be our jobs."

Burns saw an opening. "Sorry, Frank, I didn't realise you worked as a surgeon at Pleasant Infirmary." When he glanced to his right, he saw Lord wince as this provoked a big laugh from the crowd.

"Seriously, these folks have come here with nothing. Nothing but their skill and talent. Bill Adams was good enough to generously supply them with a house. A house that they only accepted after an agreement was reached – at their insistence, not Bill's – about how they would pay him back. A house that was vandalised the other evening by cowards creeping about in the dark, while two frightened young children were inside. Do we think that's okay, Arthur?"

"No, but…"

"No, of course we don't. We take great pride in the way we care and show compassion for all children. Not just our own. Not just in the great way that Graham Moore shows respect for his kid, but for the way he, and the rest of us here in Gràdh, show concern for all children. The way we show concern for all people." The youths and Bill Adams again broke into applause.

"But, good people of Gràdh, let me be crystal clear on one thing: my stance is non-negotiable. I won't chase your vote by pandering to any mob. I won't change my beliefs in the hope that you send me to Westminster. Whether you vote for me on Thursday week, or otherwise, I will always raise my voice when and wherever I find intolerance. I hope you'll join me. Thank you."

There was a fresh outburst of spontaneous and enthusiastic applause from 'the five' and some polite applause from the back of the hall, before the crowd turned and headed for the exit.

Samantha Munn moved forward and thanked Burns for his appearance, before heading quickly in the direction of Lord, who appeared to be remonstrating with a party member. Burns walked down the opposite stairs from the stage and was congratulated by his 'supporters'. Bill Adams shook him warmly by the hand.

"Bloody hell, Bill."

"What?"

"What you said to Lord. Does this mean *I* can count on your vote?"

Adams laughed heartily. "Definitely. The first time ever for your mob."

"Wow. I am flattered."

"Don't get too cocky. I'd vote for a bloody sheep before I'd vote for that clown."

Grant Moore then introduced his fellow students to Sean Burns.

"I, we, thought you were great up there. Not just today. All the way through the campaign."

Burns smiled. "I could get used to this. That's the second time in a matter of minutes that I've been flattered. I'm really grateful for all your support."

One of Moore's friends spoke. "But we can't vote – we're only seventeen."

"Not this time, that's true. But one day you will. In the meantime, as I say, your support really is appreciated." The young men talked some more about their own beliefs and concerns, before deciding to head off. Once again, they shook Sean Burns warmly by the hand and began to leave. Burns called after, then walked towards Grant Moore. "You remember last year? The terrible November snow?" Grant nodded. "Well, cars were really struggling to get across Maiden Way. The ice was terrible. When I came across the scene, four cars were already there struggling to make any sort of headway. There were other people about, but only one man was helping when I went over to push one of the cars."

"My dad?"

"I hope so, or what the hell is the point of this story?" Burns smiled, while Grant dissolved with laughter.

"Yeah. Your dad. Now I know you're probably going to say that he's got some sort of Mussolini-esque wish for transport running on time, but he *is* a good neighbour. Like a few others, he's just lost his way a little."

"I know but marching against these poor folk… it's terrible."

"I know it is. But he'll be frightened of something: his job, his house, the future." He nodded towards Lord, who was talking alone with the Headteacher. "It's what guys like him do so well: work on people's fears. Their worries. We need to argue convincingly and reassure. But, Grant, when you wake up a week on Friday – regardless of the result – you'll still be father and son."

Moore nodded earnestly to show that he understood. The two shook hands and the younger man ran off after his group of friends. Bill Adams came alongside Burns. "I suppose there's still a chance for this place with young men like that."

Burns turned to his friend. "Fingers crossed."

He then noticed that the discussion between Munn and Lord had broken up and Lord was heading for the exit. Burns called after him. "Thomas?"

Lord stopped in his tracks and turned around. "Sean?"

"Thanks for waiting for me. It was much appreciated."

Lord smiled towards his rival. "My pleasure." He then turned back and continued on his original 'path', mouthing an oath as he went. He didn't need to see the two men's faces behind him, to know that they were grinning at his discomfort.

Chapter Twenty-One

He stood gazing out of the kitchen window. All ahead was darkness. Why did she have to answer him about the election? Surely he had a right to hear from her on just who she had voted for? He knew who it would have been anyway. Him! Surely then she could have just said his name, rather than make some jokey comment about the privacy of the ballot box. Suddenly, he was catapulted out of his thoughts by the sudden loud banging of the front door.

Chapter Twenty-Two

Wednesday

David Tait stood and watched as the train pulled out of Gràdh station. He kept looking down the line after it had long vanished from sight. He'd felt this way all those years ago when Carol Ann Love had done what she had done. No, this was worse. Or was it just fresher in the mind? He hoped that Jillian Gibb and her mother would find some sort of answer at the other end of the line. Maybe he should jump on the next train and see if he could rid himself of this place? He wouldn't, though.

He knew that.

At first, when he was younger, he said that – and he believed it, too – you didn't improve things by running away. You stayed. You fought your corner. Then, through reasoning, things changed. People changed. But they didn't. He thought he had 'won' that day on the descent to Gràdh. Puffing on a cigar because he had outwitted his ex-wife and her new husband. Holding the lighter that belonged to his own father, he'd savoured the moment as a victory. A victory for… for what? Good? Decency?

Something like that. Yet here we were, years later, apparently no better. None the wiser. Sad, really.

He sighed audibly, then forced himself from his sentry position. As he made his way under the stone archway leading to the car park, he veered slightly to the right, stopping at the waste-paper bin. He took one last look at Jeff Osbourne smiling broadly up at him from underneath *The Post*'s front page and the headline *Together Again*. He threw the newspaper into the bin; but, for the second time that morning, he didn't immediately move away. It was the woman in the photograph he couldn't leave. He couldn't desert her. She might have been sitting on the floor between that psychopath Osbourne's knees and grinning – but something wasn't right. It was the eyes. They told the story. The real story. He couldn't drag himself away from Alana's eyes looking pleadingly at him. In fact, had it not been for a fellow villager heading onto the platform and shouting a 'morning' greeting towards him, he felt he might never have moved.

He was still in something of a dream state when he arrived at his car. He began to climb into the driver's seat, but then seemed to think better of it and stood once again on the tarmacadam, while he took off his brown leather jacket. As he threw it in and across to the vacant passenger seat on the left-hand side, he again hesitated, before slowly standing up to his full height. He had spotted someone, who had become an all too familiar figure around Gràdh recently, alight from the back of a private taxi cab and head inside the station.

Monday

He sat nervously stirring his spoon inside his cappuccino cup. His world had been turned upside down the previous Friday. The election, the press, the campaign, the death of his father, even the current tense situation in Gràdh, he could cope with. In fact, he had approached each and all of these difficulties head-on as his father had taught him. He had seen all of it – no matter how wearying – as a challenge. If he couldn't stand up to these *difficulties*, then how could he be expected to stand up for *all* of the people of Gràdh? But Friday? Bang. He knew she'd been worried. Worried for him. All this paper talk. It had made her nervous. Scared. For him. He looked out from the window booth at all the people milling about outside. She wasn't one of them. He'd contacted her so many times since Friday, but she'd only answered once, and that was to briefly tell him not to contact her again. She wasn't answering now. He'd texted her in desperation, asking her to meet him today. Now. But she wasn't coming. He didn't really believe that she would. Just hoped. He would have gone round to that house. But he was worried. Scared. For her.

All eyes followed her as she made her way down the aisle of the service room in the small funeral home. News travelled fast in Gràdh. Good as well as bad. But mostly bad. The word was out, and the small gathering was now here to bury a King, not pillory a paedophile. There had been little grief when the news came through to the streets and pubs that Saturday that *the pervert that had interfered with that small, innocent girl had died.* Killed himself. If that wasn't a sign of guilt, then what was? Then the news – the other news – had started to trickle through. That Jillian Gibb had retracted her statement. Had actually gone to the police station on the Saturday. Had to wait several hours before anyone could see her – they'd all been attending at the scene of the 'accident'. The terrible *accident* of poor Mr King. Too late to right the wrong.

The cumulative beast that was the good people of Gràdh didn't wallow long in any wrongdoing that may have occurred on their part; they simply moved along to the next prey: Samantha Munn. And here she was. Everyone behind her, their eyes boring into her skull. If they were hoping for some sort of reaction from her, they would be disappointed. She sat eyes directly ahead as she listened to the Humanist talk about a man she obviously didn't know. Unblinking. Unmoved. Steady as a surgeon's scalpel.

Later, when David Tait glanced towards her at the graveside, he felt a grudging respect at her stoical appearance. She knew what everyone was saying, now that the truth was out. If they were unsure about it in anyway, the giant lettering on the front of today's *Post* left no one in any doubt about where the blame lay: **School of Death!**

That had been the big surprise for Tait. Not the headline, nor the grim tale of an innocent man driven out of his mind so badly that he had decided to take his own life. No, it was the fact that his ex-wife had been so easily blindsided by Dyer. Hadn't she spotted the similarities that he had? Maybe she had, and that was both the attraction and the reason that had caused her to drop her guard. Still, it wasn't like her. Maybe she was just like the rest of us, he thought: getting older and losing the powers that she once had. Her brother Kevin nudged Tait, nodded towards her and mouthed the word "Bitch".

When the service ended, Tait allowed his three companions – who had stood at the back of the gathering – to wander ahead towards Bill Adams' car, but he stopped at the end of the pebbled pathway and waited for the rest of the mourners to pass him. Most nodded in his direction when passing, but Albert Steele stopped alongside him.

"Terrible business."

"His death, or the *Post*'s front page?"

Steele glared back at him. He had not been spared in the article. Though Dyer knew little about specific meetings from within the building, there was a quote from an Anna Caldwell, whose daughter Lisa attended the school, and she was scathing about the senior management team – particularly Steele and Lyon. Not only that, at the foot of the column there was the promise of more to come in the form of an in-depth interview with the aforementioned Mrs Caldwell. Steele leaned forward for a few seconds, as if he was about to say something, but he caught himself. Before both he and his wife, who was holding onto his arm, could move off, Tait spoke.

"You went back a long way, Bert. With Duncan, I mean."

Steele went to move away, but his wife was listening to Tait. After what seemed – to her – an unreasonable amount of hesitancy, the husband nodded.

"And you never guessed that he was gay?"

Steele began to move away again, then tried to speak, but no words could be heard.

"That's a pity, because that little bit of knowledge and understanding from a friend might just have saved him." Then Tait moved off, because he saw someone else that he wanted to speak to, but he had already passed him and was moving speedily to his car.

Tait called after him. "Brian."

Brian Gillespie looked genuinely upset and was searching frantically in his coat pockets, presumably for the keys to his Rover MG-TF.

"I can't stop. I'm in a hurry."

"That's okay, Mr Gillespie. I take it you're going to The Village?"

"No. I'm going through to Edinburgh. My wife's waiting for me." He finally retrieved his keys and climbed into the driver's seat. He started up the engine and turned back to close his door but found that David Tait had positioned himself in front of the open access point. "Look, I'm in a hurry. I told you…"

"I won't keep you, Mr Gillespie. I just want you to know…"

"And I've told *you*, I'm in a hurry."

Tait ignored the interruption. "I just want you to know that I was there. With Jillian Gibb. At the police station."

Gillespie looked impatiently towards his windscreen. "I know that." He looked up at Tait. "I heard that she'd said that nothing happened with Dunc."

Tait nodded.

"It's terrible, just terrible."

"It is. A real tragedy for all involved."

Gillespie nodded, hoping that the conversation was at an end, but Tait held his ground. "You know what I'd do if I was you?"

The man in the car looked at Tait warily now. "No, I don't. What would the guttersnipe standing before me do if he was me?"

"He'd get a good lawyer."

Gillespie's face was red now, but the charade went on. "And why, you piece of shit...?"

"Because the cops think that Jillian only lied about the name of the person that had sex with her. Not about the act itself. They're pretty sure about that."

"Look, Tait, I've lost a good friend..."

"Have you? I know that's how Dunc considered you."

"Yes, well, I felt the same."

"Then do the decent thing. It's not too late."

"You've got the wrong end of the stick."

"Have I? The vultures will be circling soon, after that story in *The Post*. There's going to be a lot of pressure on your bosses; on the cops. Might be best for you and your family if you act first." Tait stood back from the car. Gillespie seemed to contemplate what the local newspaper man had said, before he stretched towards the handle and pulled the door closed with a bang.

Tait watched him drive off. Out the corner of his eye, he saw Bill Adams and Sean Burns walking slowly, in deep conversation. He stopped at his own car and looked back towards the triangle of Thomas Lord, Tom Barker and Samantha Munn. You really didn't need to be an expert in body language to understand what was going on. Lord was speaking: delivering the *news*. Barker was staring at the ground: avoiding any gaze she might suddenly flash in his direction. And Munn? Well, she was just Samantha: tough, unbowed. She was listening intently to every word that Lord was imparting. Unflinching. The group broke up as Lord moved to hand press one of his business buddies. Barker didn't hang around. He turned immediately on Lord's departure and scurried off in the direction of his wife, who was still standing by the side of the grave. The Queen is dead. Surely? Just then, his ex-wife looked up and caught his eye.

She walked towards him as if she had something to say. She had.

"Gloating?"

He shook his head.

"Not even an, *I told you so*?"

"What is there to say to Gràdh's Daisy Buchanan?"

"But you will continue to write, I suppose?"

"Yes. I'll contact you for a quote, of course, but no doubt you'll decline. As usual."

"Well, you're wrong – this time. That's why I came over. I realise you saw our little group discussion just now, and I'm sure you can guess as to what was being said."

Tait nodded.

"Well, nothing will happen until the end of the week. We're closed for the election on Thursday. Would you come to the school on Friday? To interview me?"

Tait nodded once again. "I'll want to know how this whole mess with Duncan King started."

This time, the Headteacher nodded. Then she turned and headed back to her car. Alone. Tait had to stop himself from feeling sorry for her. A quick look across to the now empty graveside quickly disabused him of that notion.

Wednesday

Tait slammed his car door shut and headed back towards the station. He stopped under the archway entrance as the man headed inside the small newsagents. A minute or so later, the man was back outside, heading towards the platform that Tait had only recently left, dragging his suitcase along by its wheels and carrying a cup of coffee. Tait began to walk quickly towards him, but then, before he had emerged from the archway, he suddenly checked himself and turned towards the rubbish bin. He pulled out his recently discarded *Post*, turned and marched towards Colin Dyer.

Chapter Twenty-Three

Jeff Osbourne opened the door calmly and stood aside as two policemen entered. They immediately saw the limp, lifeless female body on the floor. Osbourne did not close the door, but turned, walked into the small kitchen and sat down on a chair. Despite the policeman, who was crouched down beside Alana, shaking his head towards his colleague, the other policeman spoke into his radio and requested paramedic as well as police back-up.

Sean Burns had found the last week a huge blur. He hadn't meant to let himself be affected so badly – that was the whole idea of the *Post* story, after all. But he had. This final week of the campaign – the most important of them all – had been a blur. Only once had he been able to speak to Alana, and that was an accidental meeting – on her part – this morning. He knew she'd vote. *Knew* it. That's why he had been the only candidate there for the polls' opening. When she passed him with that vicious, vindictive clown at three minutes past seven – on the way in and out of the Polling Station – he'd been careful not to provoke anything that would have meant serious repercussions for her. So he simply smiled and offered a "Good Morning" to both people: on the way in, on the way out. For a little while afterwards, he was somewhere approaching happiness, because he still saw that same look he had always seen in her eyes. The why was no longer important. He *knew*. She was doing this for *him*. Why hadn't he understood before? It didn't matter. He hoped it didn't matter. When the night was over, regardless of the result, the campaign, to bring her home, would begin.

Neighbours stood as close to *the* house as the police cordon would allow. Various groups of police milled around the entrance to Osbourne's house, while others swarmed inside. After a while, and in complete silence, Jeff Osbourne was himself led from his home by two police officers. He was helped into the back of a waiting police van, which then drove off at great speed.

Burns was suddenly aware that everyone on stage, and most of the people in the school assembly hall, were looking at him, expecting him to speak. At first, he wasn't going to say anything, let the silence speak for itself. But then, he looked from the stage and spotted Grant Moore applauding enthusiastically. Not only that, his father, standing behind him and next to the Doctors Azmeh, was also clapping loudly. Then he heard Bill Adams shout, "C'mon, Sean. Let's hear you." Encouraged, he looked around the large room – but *she* wasn't there. Slowly, he stepped forward and spoke into the microphone.

"Four votes doesn't seem much – but it's enough. Enough to ensure that we have a chosen representative at Westminster to represent *all* of Gràdh. Today's vote also tells us that we have – despite what English newspapers might tell us – an electorate that listens to the argument. An electorate – and a community – that is not governed by gossip. An electorate – and a community – that refuses to be motivated by hate. An electorate – and a community – that realises that bigotry and intolerance have no place in our society and no place in this country of ours. Ours. Our village. Our country. Our responsibility. This vote has shown that we won't use, we will not accept, those views that preach hatred and division. No. We have sounded one almighty argument today against those who wish to cloud us and confuse us over the most basic human rights issues. We are here, and we are an open village. Open to all."

This time, the applause rang out throughout the hall. Just as Sean Burns held up his hand to ask for quiet, the blood in his body ran ice cold as he spotted a worried-looking David Tait burst through the doors at the back of the hall. With a not inconsiderable effort, he turned back to the gathering, then glanced in the direction of his opponent, who stood behind his left shoulder.

"Good people of Gràdh. I congratulate Thomas Lord on his victory tonight." Some hostile noise was heard from the front of the platform, but again Burns raised his hand to plead for quiet. "Thomas, good luck in Westminster. I genuinely wish you every success, but please be aware that all of Gràdh – including our future voters – are watching you. Closely." At that, the vast majority of the hall erupted in cheers and applause. However, Burns' attention was already focused on David Tait, who now stood forlornly at the side of the stage.

Chapter Twenty-Four

Wednesday

He was almost upon the other man before he turned around. Although surprised, Colin Dyer allowed himself to break into a huge grin as he noticed Tait approaching, carrying a copy of the day's *Post*. "Good read?"

The local newspaper man reminded himself of the type of character he was dealing with and attempted to compose himself. "As ever. You not hanging around for the finale?"

Dyer beamed triumphantly. "As a wise man once said, 'My work here is done.' Besides, I don't really care who wins the election. It's not the real reason I'm here."

"I wasn't talking about the election. I'm talking about Alana Osbourne."

"Her? Hey, it's a world full of choice, and she chose hubby Jeff."

"Did she? Or did some unscrupulous prick whisper in her ear that her going back to him would help ease the pressure on Sean Burns? That sadistic bastard – hubby Jeff – laid her up in the hospital for a week last time. Fancy a bet that maybe he'll finish the job next time?"

Dyer thought for a moment that the older man was going to strike him. Behind him, he heard the sound of his train approaching. He half turned towards it. "He's had help…"

Tait walked behind him as he moved in the direction of a carriage door. Two people alighted from the single access, and Dyer leaned forward to enter. He had his right foot on the floor of the train when Tait spoke.

"Justin phoned me, you know."

Dyer's left foot seemed to hang in mid-air for a few moments, then touched back down on the platform surface, as he turned to face Tait. Now it was the turn of the Gràdh man to flash a sardonic grin.

"C'mon, don't be surprised. Your mannerisms; the way you move. You're his double." Dyer saw that the guard from his train had re-emerged from the coffee shop, carrying two cups and heading towards the front of the train and the driver's window. He shrugged.

"Yeah, just out of the blue, he phoned me. Apologised for everything. He was still under the illusion that he had picked Samantha: the wife that dumped him – another one of your victims."

Now feeling uncomfortable, Dyer was relieved to see that one coffee cup had been delivered and the guard was now walking alongside the train in his direction.

"Thankfully, he'd long since realised that the day he'd set up home with my wife was a day of huge relief for me."

Dyer attempted to look composed.

"That wasn't what he was phoning about, though."

The London man didn't know why, he just knew that he didn't want to hear any more.

"No, he wanted me to know that he was ashamed of the type of newsman he'd become."

Dyer sighed and turned once more towards the door of the train.

"Said that it was important. To him. That I knew." The other man shook his head and tried to step fully onto the train, but Tait grabbed onto his left arm and held him tight. "That I knew that he was determined to prove he was a proper journalist. That he was onto something huge. But it was the story that had to be told. The story was what was important – not him."

Dyer attempted to brush Tait off and continue on his journey, but the grip was vice-like.

"Just about ready, gentlemen," the guard, who had spotted the pair, shouted towards them from the platform at the rear of the train. Tait released him from his hold, but the younger man stood transfixed.

"It's your paper."

Dyer shook his head.

"Yes. Your paper and high-ranking cops and politicians. A cover-up."

Dyer shrugged. "Ha. What's this? A little man from a little village's fantasy."

"Not according to your uncle. That football disaster in Yorkshire six years ago. Remember who your guys blamed?"

Dyer now stared in disbelief. "It can't be…"

"That's right, Mr Dyer. The same newspaper that Bobby Burns wouldn't stock after its coverage of the disaster. The father of Sean Burns. Ironic, isn't it? Your uncle – the one you came to avenge – was on the same side as the man whose son you've come to destroy."

Dyer was shaking his head – slowly now. Disbelievingly. "Why didn't you…?"

"Say anything? Because I stupidly gave my word to Sean Burns that I wouldn't do or say anything until the votes were in. He didn't want the result tainted – regardless of the way the votes went. Then I saw you just now: scurrying away – damage done. You're a credit to *The Post*, Mr Dyer."

Suddenly, a high-pitched automatic sound came from the train and the doors began to close. Tait abruptly pushed Dyer, who stumbled backwards over the single step leading onto the train. He ended up on his backside as his trailing right leg prevented the door from closing. Before he could pull it inside, and just before the door closed, Tait leant forward and threw his copy of the day's *Post* onto the crumpled man's chest.

"And take this shit with you."

Tuesday

The four men stood in silence opposite *The Village*. Sean Burns realised that the main reason for the group's solemn demeanour was down to him. Kevin Munn in particular gave the impression that he was bursting to speak. He looked serious enough, but he kept fidgeting, as if he had some important gossip to impart, but, because of Sean's 'situation', he obviously thought that it was best kept to himself.

"Look, guys, stop ignoring the herd of elephants in the room. I know you know about Alana."

On cue, Kevin Munn, Bill Adams and David Tait looked down in the direction of their feet.

"I'm fine now. My head has been all over the place since she left, but not any more. Darkest before dawn and all that."

Bill Adams spoke for the other three. "Sean, we're here for you. If you need us to go down and see this guy, then..."

Burns smiled and shook his head. "No, I don't, Bill. But thank you. Thanks all of you. I'm not going to contact her for a couple of days, but I'll see her when she comes to vote, and..."

This time, David Tait spoke up. "Do you think he'll allow her?"

"Definitely. It'll be his way of showing that he's in charge of the situation. His way of showing me that he *owns* her."

Kevin Munn seemed unsure. "You'll need to be careful, Sean."

"Don't worry, I've no intention of starting anything there. I know that would just make things worse for her when they get back ho... to his place. Anyway, when I see her, I'll know."

"Know what?" Kevin Munn seemed perplexed.

"That she still loves me. Then, on Friday, I *am* going round to where she lives now and bring her home."

The other men seemed pleased at this. Bill Adams again offered his support. "I'm coming, too." He saw Burns about to protest. "Just in case. I'll wait in the car. A witness if you like."

Burns didn't seem overly keen on the idea, but he smiled anyway and thanked the businessman once again. "I appreciate it, Bill. I really do." He then looked at all three men. "Anyway, what I'm trying to say is that I'm better now. Much better.

I'm gonna give Tommy boy a run for his money over the next two days; and then... then I'm bringing Alana home."

David Tait patted him on the upper left arm. "Good. Very good. I'm glad to hear it."

"Right, enough about me. C'mon, Kevin. Unless I've completely lost any semblance of reality and can no longer understand people, you've got something to say."

Munn laughed. "Jesus, Sean, you're good. If only I was able to vote for you tomorrow."

His words had the desired effect, as all three men dissolved into fits of laughter. Munn then positioned himself in front of the other three men and raised his right arm grandly, calling for hush. "Gentlemen, you are now standing on the site of Gràdh's new luxury Munn Hotel. In fact, it would be more accurate to say that you are standing on the site of the hotel's extravagant bar and lounge." The other men stopped smiling and looked over Munn's shoulder towards *The Village*.

Bill Adams asked the question that was on everyone's lips. "You've got planning permission?"

"Well, to be honest, our fine councillors and townsfolk weren't too keen at first – at least regarding the lounge and bar. But I got a phone call last night. Apparently, the landlady has had a little negative publicity in the national press, and, well, they think now that, at the very least, she should enjoy a little healthy competition." He turned away and looked at the place that he once called *home*.

From over Kevin Munn's shoulder, David Tait asked a question to which he was pretty sure he already knew the answer. "What's the bar going to be called, Kevin?"

His friend closed his eyes and smiled at the memory of his father and mother in their pomp, serving the regulars in the busy village bar. He opened them again and thought of the day that had plunged the family into darkness: his father and sister arguing, and then the horrible thumping noise as his father had plunged down the stairs, followed by the even more horrendous silence. No one held her responsible; no matter what he had said. So, eventually, he had moved away. First to university; then onto various successful business adventures. He visited, but only fleetingly. He didn't want his 'new' family contaminated by staying in this place too long. He continued to help his mother: with money and staff to help keep the old place running. Then the old lady had a heart attack. He'd rushed to her bedside and was met by his sister, who 'dropped' their mother's signing over of *The Village* to her in the same sentence as she told him that their mother had died – in great pain. It had been close – very close – but he had made it. He closed his eyes again.

"Kevin? The name?"

Munn still looked straight ahead. "No secret, David. It couldn't really be anything else, could it?"

Now he turned to face the other three.

"Sheila's."

David Tait watched Jillian Gibb's mother rise from the kitchen table and walk over to the open door. "Jillian, love. It's Mr Tait, here to see you."

Almost immediately, Tait heard the girl moving directly above him. A good sign, he hoped. Seconds later, the girl was in the small kitchen, and – as David Tait rose from his seat – she rushed towards him, hugging him warmly, for some considerable time. Eventually, she broke away and sat down on a third chair, on Tait's left, positioned in the centre of the square table. As she did so, her mother, who had sat down opposite Tait again, stood and walked over to the sink and began to fill a silver kettle with cold water from the tap. Jillian, who was now nervously wringing her hands and staring at the table, looked up slowly at Tait.

"Mum told you?" The newspaper man nodded. "You must hate me?"

Tait reached over the kitchen table and placed his right hand between hers – any feeling of possible impropriety had long since passed. Her two hands squeezed his gently.

"You know something, Jillian? I've thought about leaving Gràdh, god, I don't know, many, many times."

"But you didn't."

He squeezed her hand reassuringly.

"No, I didn't. The first few times – when my wife at the time was encouraging me – it was because I thought I had vital work to do here. Later, when I found many things here that were ugly and deplorable, I found myself thinking back to the advice my mother had once given me. She had warned me that I shouldn't ever think that running away ever solved anything. My father was the same: if you wanted change, then you had to do it from within. In more recent times, I've found inspiration from good people like Ian Moyes and Bobby Burns – and now his son Sean. They have made me believe in people. Made me believe that *we* could win."

The young girl looked distraught and released his hand from her grasp. "So you are angry?"

Tait laughed gently and brought both his hands lightly upon hers.

"Not in the least. I think all I was doing – all these different times – was doing what I wanted. I wasn't being brave. I wasn't being noble. Maybe I was scared. Maybe I was lazy. To be honest, I don't really know why. But I do know that I stayed. It was my decision. Made many times over the years.

Whatever the reason: I stayed. Why shouldn't you do what you – and your mum – think is right?"

Mrs Gibb walked across to the couple, smiled and laid down two piping hot mugs of tea in front of them both.

"Tell you what, ladies, I'll even run you both down to the station. How's that?"

Tait noticed that when the young girl turned to her smiling mother, she had a relieved look on her face. He didn't know why, but it made him feel a little sad that, even after all she had been through, she had still sought his approval. But then maybe that really was the final proof that she should get as far away from Gràdh as possible.

Wednesday

After an emotional goodbye, Jillian made her way inside the train carriage. Mrs Gibb lingered on the platform, before turning back to Tait. "I know you're fond of Jillian, but I genuinely hope that you can find it in your heart to forgive me. You must think…"

"Genuinely, there is nothing to forgive, Mrs Gibb. You could stay looking for justice and never find it – damaging Jillian along the way. Take their money. Start a new life."

She turned and climbed the one step onto the

train. She smiled back at him. "It's a big, wide world out there."

He smiled back. "So they tell me."

Chapter Twenty-Five

Friday: Early Hours

David Tait reacted with a start as his phone vibrated. It was the second time Kevin Munn had contacted him in the last few hours. The first time had been to find out the result of the previous night's election. Kevin hadn't been overly optimistic that Sean Burns would win, but he hoped that he would. He'd always been fond of the man's father, Bobby Burns, who had been particularly kind to him when his own father had passed. Not only that, but two of his oldest friends – David Tait and Bill Adams – couldn't speak highly enough of the younger man. However, when Tait had answered his call earlier, he hadn't just discovered the election result. Now he was phoning to see how Burns was. Tait and Adams had insisted on coming back to his flat with him, and Burns, seeing that they had no intention of leaving him alone, despite his pleas, had retreated to his bedroom, while the two men kept vigil, sitting slumped on two chairs in the small lounge of Burns' flat. As Tait quietly related the whole sorry tale to his friend over his mobile phone, Bill Adams stood and stretched, before walking into the kitchen and filling the kettle. When the telephone conversation had ended, he entered the lounge and handed Tait one of the two hot mugs of coffee that he was carrying and sat down opposite the other man. For a moment it looked as if he would say something, but then he just shrugged and sat further back in the chair. Tait nodded sadly towards him. He understood there was nothing to say. There were no words.

Thursday

The candidates had been around Gràdh's Polling Station – and High School – most of the day. Derek and Deborah Lord had arrived at the Village Hall – where the votes were being counted and where the result would be announced – around 10.45 p.m. The count, despite Gràdh's growth in recent years, would still be a relatively quick one. When the candidate emerged from the back seat of the vehicle, he was holding his cellphone to his ear.

"Thank you, Mr Swain. I appreciate that – and all your support... Sir Reginald did?... Fantastic... No, we'd all be disappointed with that."

Inside, Bill Adams stood chatting with David Tait, when they were joined by a beaming Sean Burns. "Hi, guys, all well?" The businessman and the 'ace' reporter from *The Gràdh and Pleasant Post* exchanged curious glances. The candidate continued, "I've never been better." Once again, the other two men looked at each other, before Adams spoke.

"Sean, has someone leaked the result or something?"

Now it was Sean Burns' turn to look puzzled. "Result? No, I haven't heard a thing."

"So?"

"Alana phoned. About an hour ago. Said she was sorry, which is daft, I know, but anyway, she said that she's coming home."

David Tait patted him warmly on his left arm. "That's great news. When?"

"She is coming down here shortly. I wanted to go and get her straight away, but she said that it wouldn't be wise. Might make things worse. With Osbourne, I mean. She's going to be here for the result being announced." Of the three men, only Bill Adams seemed concerned.

"Sean, I…"

"I know, Bill. It might not be an easy subject to broach with Osbourne. She said that herself. If he's volatile, or she senses something, she'll have dinner as usual with him and text me that she can't get away. Once the result's done and dusted, I'll head down to the house myself and get her." He had just completed his sentence when a constituent stepped forward and introduced himself. Adams and Tait smiled and shuffled away from the conversation.

"I don't like it, David. That Osbourne's a nutter. Or whatever the correct technical term is."

"No, you're right, it's a worry. I'm certainly not for Sean going down to get Alana on his own."

"We'll go, eh? I know the big cop at the other side of the hall. I'll have a word with him, too. See if we can get a couple of the boys in blue to join us. Make sure everything is done properly. No loose ends."

Tait nodded. "Let's see if she appears – or at least texts him. In fact, I'll head down there before the vote is announced; keep an eye on the place. Just in case."

Adams smiled. "Definitely, David. That's a good idea. I feel a bit more reassured now."

Friday: Morning

Bill Adams stood outside the entrance to the block of flats, deep in conversation with Kevin Munn, passing on what information he had: no text messages had come from Alana; concerned, Sean had texted her – nothing; time had passed; more concerned, Sean had tried phoning Alana; when he had begun to get anxious, David had gone to check; police and paramedics already there. Two floors above them, the shell of Sean Burns stared blankly, silently out of the window.

David Tait sat a second boiling hot mug of tea – coffee had also already been spurned – on the sunken wooden table a few feet behind where Burns stood. He picked up the full, cold, untouched mug that had lain in the same spot for an hour. He was heading back in the direction of the kitchen when he stopped and turned around. "I told you Harry from the local office and Gerry from the national office had phoned. Both were very upset." Nothing. He tried again. "Told you Tommy Jacobs had phoned in person. Early this morning. As soon as he heard. Seems a good bloke. Anything you need, he said." Tait waited until a few seconds had elapsed, then headed back noiselessly towards the kitchen.

Thursday

A more content Bill Adams swung around, straight into the ebullient figure of Thomas Lord. His wife, who had arrived in the hall with him, was off to his left, charming some supporters. "Come on, Bill. Admit it. You voted for me when you went into that booth, didn't you? Profit over conscience, eh?"

With all the concern about Alana, Adams, usually never short of a quip, was caught on the hop for once. Lord laughed out loud, then smirked as he eased himself past the businessman. He had only gone another two steps when Adams snapped out of his trance and called after the once-upon-a-time, and now would-be, Member of Parliament.

"Do you still think of her, Thomas?"

Lord was still facing away from Adams, but he had stopped.

"Well, do you, Thomas?"

Lord finished speaking to a rotund and florid-looking male before he turned around and – wearing a fixed smile – took a step back towards Adams.

"Who?"

"Carol Ann."

Lord looked more confused than surprised.

"Carol Ann Love. You do remember her?"

Lord was oblivious of anything going on around him at that moment. He had stopped smiling and his eyes seemed to have glazed over. Like a prize-fighter who had been caught by a sucker punch, he instinctively understood that he was in trouble and that now was a time for survival. He began to turn away, but Adams 'caught' him again.

"Helluva shock that day. For Ian Moyes and Bobby Burns, I mean. "The two men were standing closely now, facing each other. "You know, Bobby Burns: Sean's dad. They all knew, Thomas."

Lord was looking disbelievingly at Adams now. "But Sean?"

"Yeah, Sean."

Suddenly, Lord's wife appeared at his side, her frozen smile suddenly disappearing. "Are you okay, darling?"

Unconvincingly, he smiled towards her and gently eased her in front of him as he returned to his original path. However, Adams held him tightly by his right arm and he half-turned to face the businessman once again.

"Don't lose any sleep or worry about any scheme or plans young Burns is concocting. It's nothing like that. It's dead simple, Thomas. There is no mystery. Just like his father before him, he's a better man than you."

With that, Adams released his grip, and Lord, shaken, continued on his way through the hall.

Friday: Afternoon

Bill Adams had returned to the flat with hot bacon rolls and some groceries that Sean Burns *might* need in the days ahead. An hour later, David Tait emerged from Burns' bedroom with the untouched rolls and another full mug of tea that he had made earlier.

"No change?"

Tait shook his head. "No. He headed back in after the cops came to speak to him earlier." After he had placed the disregarded foodstuff in the kitchen, Tait returned and sat down opposite Bill Adams. "Poor Sean."

Adams looked at the other man and realised that as well as being concerned for his friend, he seemed troubled, too.

"You know, David, I've been going over this whole thing in my mind: could I have done this, could I have done that? Maybe I should've pressed Sean more when he said he would handle it his own way. Christ, I've made a great job of looking after him for his father. But his dad, and Sean himself, they know their own minds. Or at least they give the impression that they do. Maybe that's some sort of self-absolution; I just don't know. I really don't. I do know that I phoned the kids first thing this morning. I just had to hear their voices. Christ, I even gave the wife a cuddle last night." Tait smiled softly. "Whatever's happened, David, we're here for him now. Don't beat yourself up."

Tait nodded but seemed unconvinced. "I should've been onto that prick Dyer earlier; but, as ever, I let things rumble on. I let the situation slide away. There's been so many people damaged by all of this. Jesus, Bill, three people have died."

"Three?"

At that moment, the flat's doorbell rang and both men leapt protectively towards the ingress. They needn't have been concerned, because when David Tait opened the door, there stood the diminutive figure of Grant Moore, holding a small but colourful bouquet of flowers.

David Tait waved the youngster quietly inside and was just about to explain to him that Sean Burns was having a 'lie down' when the figure of the object they were about to discuss appeared at the lounge door. Despite his dazed expression, Burns insisted that the younger man sit down for a cup of tea. It was Bill Adams' turn now to insist that Burns should also sit down and he would go and put on the kettle for what seemed like the one hundredth time that morning.

When all four men had sat down, the repetitious routine of the last several hours was continued: three of the men sipped tea and made small, small talk, while Sean Burns stared absent-mindedly towards the ground. After about thirty minutes, both Tait and Moore indicated that they would have to go. They mumbled their goodbyes towards Burns and stood up. Bill Adams pointed his finger towards the youngster's left temple.

"Grant, what's that?"

The youngster put his index finger towards it and held out his left hand to let everyone see some dried-up magnolia-coloured paint.

"How'd you get that?"

"Well, someone had defaced the Azmehs' house again." He looked at Burns and his voice trailed off. "The morning of the election…" He nodded towards the other three men and began to head towards the door. More out of an attempt to break the surrounding silence than anything else, Bill Adams spoke again.

"I saw that. You did well."

Then, almost as an afterthought, David Tait spoke while putting on his jacket at the front door. "I thought you weren't going down there until this afternoon?"

"I wasn't. But when I was driving past with my dad this morning, I saw that this guy had already started, so I got my dad to pull over and I went to give him a hand."

Bill Adams looked at the youngster quizzically. "One of your pals, was it?"

"No, it wasn't. I got a bit of a shock, to be honest."

Adams and Tait exchanged a bewildered glance, before speaking in unison. "Who was it?"

"Thomas Lord."

The two older men were struck dumb, and for several seconds silence again dominated. Then Grant Moore opened the flat's door and turned to say his final farewell. "You know *him*, probably just some publicity stunt. I certainly won't be mentioning it to anyone else." The two men, still appearing confused, nodded in his direction. Moore turned and was just about to move off when a voice came from behind Adams and Tait.

"Grant. Thanks for coming around. And thanks for the flowers. I really appreciate it." The youngster nodded, but Burns hadn't quite finished. It was as if Moore's revelation regarding Lord had acted like a bucket of ice-cold water across his face. He was alert. Wounded, hurt, but alive once again. "And Grant. Lord's done a good thing here. Tell everyone you meet. He's done well. It's only fair."

With that, young Moore headed downstairs.

"Right, you two. I'm going for a shower. See if I can feel a bit more human."

The two men nodded towards each other, then Adams accompanied his friend downstairs. They stood outside the front door of the entrance to the block of flats, taking in the welcome fresh air. David Tait glanced behind him. "Good to see him up and about. It's a long way to go – but it is encouraging."

Adams nodded. "Yeah. He'll get there."

Tait then stepped slowly down the three steps which took him onto the pavement and towards where his car sat. Adams called after him. "David, you said earlier that three people had died. Alana and King? Who else were you thinking of: Bobby Burns?"

"No. I meant Carol Ann Love. But hey, this place has claimed so many. Poor Kevin is going to be next. Hell, maybe this goes right back to his dad, Frank."

Adams seemed deflated. "Yeah. Maybe you're right. Maybe it is this place. Christ, a serial killer couldn't have done a better job."

Tait had now opened the driver's door and grinned sardonically towards the businessman. "Funnily enough, I'm just on my way to interview the nearest thing we have to Peter Manuel." With that, he slid inside, started the engine and drove off, waving to Bill Adams, who turned and, with a sigh, made his way back to his sad vigil.

Chapter Twenty-Six

It wasn't yesterday that he'd attended, but he remembered that this was the time when school was truly *silent*. Ten past nine. As long as it started at nine, of course. So many moments in his life had been forgotten or had become foggy. Not this. There would be a constant cacophony of noise in the corridors as pupils – or were they students now? – made their way to the various classes. The wailing would gradually drop to a murmur as they entered their classroom. The transformation from sound to silence was not instant. Chairs would be moved; desks would be pulled backwards and forwards on the bare wooden floor. Registers taken, and then faraway footsteps of the stragglers could be heard. Then – by ten past nine – when the last corridor had given up its last child and the last door had been pulled shut, there was a harmonious silence. Those moments the teacher had to savour, for eventually the beasts would rise from their slumber and the battle would recommence. Tait smiled to himself at the memory as he listened to the sound of his own footsteps. Not immediately, but he heard the rhythm intensify and realised the beat was also being kept by someone else walking in his direction. He began considering how to greet Brian Gillespie as soon as he recognised the man approaching. However, the concern was short-lived, as Gillespie, staring straight ahead, marched past Tait and continued on his way to the exit without breaking stride.

When he reached Miss Grace's office, he thought that maybe the school, sensibly under the circumstances, had decided to maintain a vow of silence as she simply waved him by, indicating that he should proceed directly to the dragon's lair. He liked that, sort of, about employees like Miss Grace – and indeed all school secretaries, doctors' receptionists and their ilk. They defended and protected their man or woman with all the ferocity of a lioness sheltering their young, but – when the time was up for the object of that protection – they moved on quickly. No looking back. No remorse.

Tait knocked on the door and entered. She was standing, back towards him, facing out of the giant window behind her desk. Gràdh's Scarlett O'Hara at her most enigmatic. Surely, this time, she knew that her reign as Queen Bee was at an end. Yet Tait knew her well. Better than anyone – though he didn't know if that was saying a great deal. Until he heard the words from her own lips, then he wasn't quite ready to prepare for the abdication. She turned around slowly.

"How are you, David? Good to see you."

Christ, this was a worse start than he had anticipated: less Queen more Thatcher style *faux* sincerity.

"I'm good. I saw Brian Gillespie on the way out. History, is he?"

There was that sad, depressed, insincere look on her face once again. She nodded slowly, signalled to him to sit on the chair on the other side of her desk, while she – slowly, painfully – lowered herself onto her own. "I've had to let him go. It wasn't working out."

"Fucking the kids? I can understand how that could be problematic. That's not part of the job description. Not in other schools, anyway."

Tait's aggressiveness caused her to flinch for a second, but years of practice saw the guarded, calm demeanour return to Samantha Munn in a heartbeat. "Is this an official enquiry about Mr Gillespie? Because if it is, I'm afraid I can only give you an official answer: he's resigned. He's upset about the death of a former colleague and has decided to take some time off to explore other options – career-wise."

"Resigned? So no extra cash, then? No little sweetener to help him on his way?"

"That is a completely private…"

"Of course. But, Samantha, just how much money does it take to send him packing – along with Jillian Gibb and her mother? And who the hell is footing the bill for all of this? I take it the puppets of the School Board have approved it?"

Samantha Munn sat upright and was preparing to launch into the *official party line*, but Tait held up his left hand: a signal for her to desist. "Of course, you'll have saved a fortune with Duncan King's suicide. Are we still calling it suicide?"

Munn shook her head. "This... this tirade is not what I've called you here for."

"No, I know. But the other day at Duncan's funeral, you said that you'd answer some questions."

"And I will. But I want to give you some positive news for a change."

Tait looked at her cautiously.

"It's about Kevin."

"Go on."

"Well, Joan came to see me and... anyway, I've been for tests and it turns out I'm a perfect match. Isn't it great?"

Tait smiled and nodded in affirmation. Of course it was great news, but...

"Apparently, this can give him a real chance. A real hope of survival. I keep thinking of him. And Fiona. And the kids, of course."

Tait nodded again. "It *is* great news." Her prodigious act of humanity had taken him aback. However, as delighted as he was for his childhood friend, he was, as ever, aware that when Samantha Munn Tait Meade Munn did something good, never mind exceptional, there was usually a reason behind it. If it was simply to make him veer from the track of discovering what had happened to make Duncan King *persona non grata* at Gràdh High School, then it was not going to work. "You're doing a good thing…"

"Thank you."

"… for a great guy. And a lovely family."

She nodded much less enthusiastically at the second part of his speech.

"Are you going to stonewall me on everything, Ms Munn? Because, honestly, I'm really not in the mood…"

"Ms Munn? C'mon, David, it's just you and I in here. I'll answer anything that I can – but off the record."

"You're not on. Too much has happened under your watch. You're finished. You must see that."

"I see that small-minded, arrogant people want me out. That's not the same thing."

"Look, that ferret-faced fraud Tom Barker will sing like a canary. The two Berts, too! Anything to save themselves."

"But they *are* safe. As long as they keep quiet, then they'll continue for as long as is necessary."

Tait realised this verbal sparring was leading nowhere. He knew that she was right. About the hush money paid out to Gillespie and the Gibbs. He was just surprised that she'd missed Mrs Caldwell. Still, even this well-to-do school probably couldn't match what *The Post* were paying. Who was going to jeopardise their own little fiefdom in return for a place in God's kingdom? Their deal had been made. They'd settled for their little bit of heaven on earth and they'd take their chances when it came time to visit the next life.

However, he wasn't going to give up on Duncan King and his good name so easily.

"Samantha. What about Duncan?"

"What about him?"

"He was a good guy. Now he's dead."

"Yes."

"Is that it?"

"Yes."

"You killed him."

"Oh, David, for fu…"

"You and your acolytes. You and your cowardly bloody disciples. You killed a good man. An innocent man."

She looked away from him. Then stared back at him.

"What was the song, Samantha? What was the song?" She still looked unperturbed. "From what I can gather – what most folk who were there on the night can actually remember – it was a medley that he played." She looked away again. He stood up. "Christ, Samantha, what was it?"

He began pacing the room as if involved in some perverse game of charades. Saying a title, then quickly dismissing it. "Okay, was it about charity? You wouldn't like that! Something condemning the rich? No? Politics? Something about... god, I don't... Family?"

Now she stood up. "Look, this is…"

A sudden realisation lit his face. "Shit. That's it. Family? No? Not specific enough..." Samantha Munn sat back down on the couch and stared, not at him, but straight ahead. *"Not just family… that one… the rock song about the little girl and her father?"* There was silence for a few moments, and they were looking at each other now. "Christ, Samantha. That was his 'crime'? He sang a song that mentioned the word *Daddy*?"

"You didn't see him."

"No, I didn't. Are you mad?"

Her voice was raised now. "You didn't see him, and you didn't see the way he looked over at me when he sang that part."

"They ought to certify you. You're crazy." She began to interrupt, but he continued, "He looked at you? Christ, he wouldn't even be able to make you out from the stage. He wouldn't know anything about Frank. Or how he died. Christ, Samantha, even for you, this is just too much. Too fucking much!"

The Headteacher had heard enough and decided to strike back, eyes ablaze. "He knew, all right. He knew. Somebody must've told him. Probably Kevin."

Tait felt incredulity sweep over him like a fever. "Kevin? In case you've forgotten, Missus Headteacher, your brother is dying; and – strange as it may seem to you – he is not spending his last days on earth pestering strangers about suspicions he has harboured about you since you were kids."

Silence reigned again.

Samantha Munn looked pleadingly at him.

"What?"

"You loved me once. Didn't you? Or did I imagine it."

Tait stood up and answered quietly. "No. You didn't imagine it. I did once. Like most of the people you've known, I fell under your spell – but only for a while." At that, he turned to leave, but she spoke and stopped him in his tracks.

"You don't know what Frank was like."

He turned and observed her for a few seconds. "No, I don't. And I'm quite happy about tha…"

"Always cuddling up to me. Kissing me."

Tait attempted to remain uninterested. "And why not? He was your father, after all."

"You don't understand. Not like a father. Not like a father at all."

Tait was staring at her now. "And the stairs?"

"It didn't take much. He was drunk. Unbalanced."

Once again, the newspaper man found himself fumbling for words. "I used to hold you so tight. Make you feel that everything was all right. Tell you that Kevin was just upset. Tell you that he'd realise one day just how wrong he'd been." He smiled ruefully at her. "Yet you knew. You knew that he was right, yet nothing. Nothing to me. Your husband."

Again he turned to leave, but again she spoke, and again he stopped, and again he turned around to face her. "You said earlier that I was finished. No way back. Well, you're wrong. There is a way I can survive this." He shifted uncomfortably. He wasn't sure why, but when Samantha Munn had a plan, it was natural to feel nervous.

He tried to speak reassuringly, but he wasn't sure if he managed to carry it off.

"I don't understand. How can you possibly survive this?"

"Marry me."

He laughed in spite of the revulsion that he felt at that moment. "Christ, Samantha. What is this? *You* left me. Yet every ten years I get a proposal from you." This time, he turned *and* headed towards her office door.

She went after him. "You said that you loved me once. For real. You could love me again."

"Humour me. How the hell would that help you stay on here in this hell-forsaken torture chamber you've created?"

She was talking excitedly now. "People will back off when they see that we're together again. They respect you. They'll think that if that 'good guy' sees something good in her, then she must be worth saving."

Tait had control of himself again. Despite his brain screaming at him to be careful. Despite his constant knowledge that you should never lower your guard against Samantha Munn.

"Please don't think me rude, Ms Munn. After all, you accepted my one proposal many, many moons ago. However, I must decline your heartfelt offer – for the second time. Please don't think badly of me." He grinned and pulled the handle of the office door towards himself.

The door was barely ajar when Samantha Munn stopped its motion by leaning against it and looking directly into Tait's eyes.

"Are you sure you won't consider it."

"Not even if it meant saving my life."

"What if it meant saving a friend's?"

Chapter Twenty-Seven

David Tait stood on the spacious lawn at the rear of Bill Adams' house. He stood alone, holding a fresh Jack Daniels on ice, staring out beyond the wooden fence, looking out at Gràdh. Not just the town, but the surrounding countryside and its *forty shades of green*. How beautiful. How ugly. Was there a curse on the place? Years ago, he would have laughed at the very thought. Not any more. All the good people seemed to leave either by dying or realising, quicker than him, what the place was really like. Yet Bill Adams was here. So was Sean Burns. And there was real hope for the future when he thought of young people like Grant Moore and his friends. Feeling better within himself, he recalled how close the election had been. Four votes. Four votes; and that was after a monumentally dirty campaign had been visited upon the tiny Scots' village by the might of the British establishment. Maybe Gràdh wasn't so ugly after all. Maybe, at some point, the people themselves, including him, had gotten complacent. They'd ignored signs that there were problems. But not now. Not now. It was the young people. They'd shown the way. They'd realised how unwelcoming the population, who had laid out the red carpet for the privileged few, had been towards the refugees and others in need. They'd realised that it wasn't right. That things had to change. And, unlike him and his fellow old fogies, who protested quietly and within the rules that no one else adhered to, they'd matched the rage of the ill-informed, ignorant zealots – for good. He smiled to himself: *bloody kids!*

Just then, a clamour from behind informed him that Kevin and Joan Munn had arrived. As they were being warmly greeted by everyone, including the hosts, Tait raised his glass in salute in the direction of Kevin, who, smiling widely, broke away from the throng and headed towards him. The two old friends shook hands, then embraced. Tait hesitated a second as he felt the sharp bones of his once well-built friend through his clothing. Hopefully, his treatment would start soon. Kevin was laughing.

"I believe congratulations are in order?"

Tait smiled awkwardly. "Yeah. Samantha tell you?"

"Oh, yeah, couldn't wait."

Sean Burns and Bill Adams had been approaching the pair, but something in the two men's body language suggested that they were in the middle of some sort of important issue. So they stopped and formed their own small group, occasionally glancing over to see when it might be appropriate to approach.

Kevin, despite his condition, seemed to be revelling in his friend's awkwardness. The newspaper man was sounding very serious and looking very sincere, he thought. He and Samantha had had many difficulties, but the time had come to work through them. He, Tait, had always loved her. She was... misunderstood. Finally, Kevin could take no more. He placed his right hand on his old pal's left shoulder.

"David, stop. Stop right there. I'm not accepting her offer of a transplant."

"But, Kevin..."

"No buts, David. There is not a cat's chance in hell that I'd ever accept anything from her. Not even one of her organs. *Especially* not one of her organs. The risk of even a tiny part of her personality seeping into my system is just too much."

"Even if it means your death?"

Kevin smiled warmly. "Even if it means my death."

Tait tried one more angle. "Christ, Kevin, I hope this isn't the second time you miss our wedding."

In the face of his own demise, the man opposite him was laughing uproariously now. He stopped and looked earnestly at Tait. "David, come on. We know each other and we both know my sister. She blackmailed you into this."

"Did she…?"

"She didn't have to. I know her. *I'll help Kevin if you help me.*"

Tait's look said it all. He nodded towards Joan. "What about her? And the kids?"

Kevin took a deep breath. "Don't think for a minute that it's easy leaving them. They are my life."

"Then…"

"No, David. The transplant is not going to happen. I'd feel that I was attaching another form of cancer to my body with a piece of that woman inside me. She's vile. Always has been."

"Maybe she's damaged, too."

"Kevin, you should know, maybe even as well as me, what that woman is like and what she's capable of." Tait tried to interrupt, but he went on. "She got my mum, on *her* deathbed, to sign over the pub to her. She killed my dad." Again, he realised that Tait was considering saying something, so he kept going. "Listen to me, David. She. Killed. Him. At first, when I used to accuse her, she used to say I was talking nonsense. Later on, when I wouldn't let it go, she'd change her story. She'd say he hated her; he beat her up. Then, when that little avenue of excuses had run into a cul-de-sac, it was abuse time. My father used to sneak into her room at night. Only problem was, she would mix up her dates. Claim it was on a night when my dad wasn't even at home. Or she wasn't there. She's evil, David: one hundred percent, pure evil."

It was difficult for Tait to argue. He certainly did not want to marry her. Once had been a disaster. Twice? She had done so many things; so many horrible things. He'd had doubts himself about her recent claim of abuse. Why? Because, when backed into a corner, she always lied. Always protected herself. Regardless of who else had been hurt.

Kevin saw that Tait may have been injured again. Just because he had given her the benefit of the doubt somewhere along the line – again.

"David, I'll never forget what you were willing to do for me. I mean that. You're a true friend. My best friend."

They embraced again and signalled towards the other two men hovering nearby to join them.

The evening was most enjoyable. Kevin Munn had joked relatively early on that it was a fantastic thing to attend one's own wake. When it came time for him to leave, David Tait wondered when, and in what condition, he would next find his friend. He did not have to wait long for an answer.

For a few moments, as the group broke up at the end of the night, Kevin and David found themselves alone again outside Adams' house. As

Joan waved from the back of the taxi cab, Tait's best friend and former brother-in-law confided in him. "I'm not saying to the rest of them, David, but I won't be back. Now, please, let me finish. I won't forget you. Not for any of the things that you've done for me over the years. This latest marriage thing; Christ, that really was over and beyond." The group, gathered at the entrance to the house, wondered what had made the two men laugh so raucously. They hugged again.

This time, the feeling of his friend's frail body against him made Tait's eyes well up. As Kevin broke away, he spoke almost conspiratorially. "Promise me one last thing."

"Anything."

Kevin Munn smiled for a moment. That's why the man opposite from him was his great friend. No hedging of bets; no hesitancy. Just an immediate, positive response. "When the new complex opens. You'll be there? It's just… Joan and the kids…"

Again the response was immediate and welcoming. "I wouldn't miss it for anything. Are you still going with the same name?"

"Sheila's? Of course." As Kevin Munn walked around the back of the cab, he continued, "What other name could it be? That woman *was* a saint."

As Tait waved off the taxi cab, he recalled what a beautiful-looking lady *the Saint* had been. A fantasy figure from his youth. He recalled how, within two months of marrying her daughter, *the Saint* had walked into his bedroom and deliberately dropped the towel that had been covering her and stood there grinning. The fantasy had become reality. Problem was that fantasy had no place in reality. He knew that. He made his displeasure known and the matter had never been mentioned again.

Another taxi cab pulled up. This one was for Tait and Sean Burns. After another round of *goodnights* with the hosts, the two men slid onto the back seat of the car. Sean Burns seemed to be coping well. He had kept himself busy, but he explained he was still 'fond' of the occasional cry. He would survive because Alana Osbourne would want him to. He would carry on his fight to make the world – and Gràdh – a better place, because Alana Osbourne would expect him to.

"Are the party members down south still calling with offers of a safe seat?"

"Not any more. I told them thanks, but I'd be working at a local level here, and then... maybe someday, I'll try again."

The taxi cab drew to a halt outside the entrance to David Tait's flat. The two men shook hands and arranged to meet up for a 'pint' during the next week. From the pavement, Tait leaned back inside the car's open door for one last farewell. "You take care, Sean. I'm glad for Gràdh that you're staying."

"Me, too. You know, David, despite everything that's happened, my overwhelming emotion is one of contentment."

Tait looked confused. "Contentment?"

Burns laughed. "Yes. God knows, there have been some bloody horror stories this past year, but I am so glad that I knew Alana. And I'm so proud that Bobby Burns was my father. And I am so glad that when this hideous year blew up in the most appalling way, all around me I discovered that I had the most wonderful, caring friends nearby, supporting me."

Tait nodded. "I'm glad, then. Goodnight, Sean."

"Goodnight, David." Then, just as Tait began to swing the door closed, Burns leaned over the seat and signalled him to wait.

"Anything is possible when you have family and friends, but we need to reach out to those who are alone."

Tait opened the door a bit wider and peered back in. "Do we?"

Burns laughed. "Of course. Somebody's got to take the first step. We can't give up on anyone. Everyone deserves an opportunity to change, or how is anything ever going to get better?"

The newspaper man nodded slowly and closed the car door. He returned a final wave towards the rear window of the taxi cab, stood for a few seconds staring into space, before heading towards the entrance to his flat.

Seven months later

"Are you sure you want to go through with this?"

"Nope. But I'm going to."

"Are you sure you don't want me to wait?"

"Yes. Thanks anyway, but I think I'll need the walk to clear my head and then I'll catch the bus back into Gràdh."

David Tait watched Sean Burns get out of the front passenger seat of the car and head towards the entrance door of East Deckert Prison. Sean had told him that he believed it would aid his own recuperation if he met Jeff Osbourne: Alana's killer – and ex-husband. Get out some of the rage that was still in him. Tait wasn't so sure of that being the reason. Not the sole reason, anyway. Tait felt that, simply put, Sean Burns was a *good guy*. Even through his ghastly connection to Osbourne, he always operated on a particular code of conduct. He always did his best. Not just for himself but for everyone else. By seeing Osbourne, he was doing the *right* thing. The *just* thing. Was he a fool? Possibly. But he knew that, in the upcoming by-election, caused by the sudden resignation of Thomas Lord, he'd happily vote for him again.

Tait's car swung lazily onto Gràdh Main Street, before finally coming to a halt outside the offices of *The Gràdh and Pleasant Post*. He sat staring at nothing in particular before his thoughts turned to people. So many people: Carol Ann Love, Justin Meade, Ian Moyes, Bobby Burns, Bill Adams, the Azmehs, Kevin Munn, Colin Dyer, Thomas Lord, Alana Osbourne, Duncan King, Jeff Osbourne, Jillian Gibb, Brian Gillespie. The list seemed endless. He thought most of all about Sean Burns. He reignited his car and turned back onto the road.

He pulled up in front of the house just as the occupant was heading for the car in the driveway. Within seconds, Tait was speeding back onto the main road – with a passenger.

"You realise I lied?"

Tait continued to look straight ahead.

"You realise that I lied – about Frank?"

This time, his eyes still on the road ahead, he allowed himself a brief nod.

When they reached their destination, Samantha Munn turned to her right and looked directly at David Tait. "If you know that I lied to you – again – then why the hell have you come along to hold my hand on my first visit to this bloody quack?"

Tait pressed off the ignition and pulled out his fob, before returning his passenger's gaze.

"Yeah, well, a wise man once told me that somebody's got to make the first move. We can't give up on anyone."

She observed him quizzically. "Yeah?"

"Yeah. Or, how is anything ever going to get better?"